THE SILKEN THREAD

BY THE SAME AUTHOR

Alberta Alone
Alberta and Freedom
Alberta and Jacob
Krane's Café: An Interior with Figures
The Leech

Cora Sandel

The Silken Thread

STORIES AND SKETCHES

TRANSLATED FROM THE NORWEGIAN
AND WITH AN INTRODUCTION BY
ELIZABETH ROKKAN

Ohio University Press
Athens, Ohio

First published in English by Peter Owen Limited 1986.
Second printing, 1988

Ohio University books are printed on acid free paper. 

Ohio University Press edition published 1987.
Printed in the United States of America.

Library of Congress Cataloging-in-Publication Data

Sandel, Cora, 1880–1974.
The silken thread.

I. Title.
PT8950.F2S5 1987 839.8′2372 86–23857
ISBN 0–8214–0864–X
ISBN 0–8214–0865–8 (pbk.)
First published in Great Britain 1986

Contents

NOTE

The years given in parentheses above are, in most cases, the first dates of publication. One exception, The Women in the Bath-house, *was written in the period 1940–45 but not published until 1973.*

Introduction

Cora Sandel is the pseudonym of Sara Fabricius, who was born in Kristiania (Oslo) in 1880. After studying to be a painter, mainly in Paris, before and during the First World War, she abandoned painting at the age of forty, settled in Sweden, and turned seriously to writing, publishing the first volume of her *Alberta* trilogy in 1926. In the decades that followed, five collections of short stories and novellas came out alternately with her novels, and both of these genres made up the six volumes of the *Collected Works* when they were published in Norway in 1952. At the age of eighty Cora Sandel was the runner-up in a European competition for her last novel, *Kjøp ikke Dondi* (The Leech), and the year before her death in 1974 a collection of texts not previously published in book form, edited by Steinar Gimnes, appeared under the title of one of the stories, chosen by Sandel, *Barnet som elsket veier* (The Child Who Loved Roads).

Sara Fabricius guarded her privacy. As women authors have in the past used male pseudonyms in order to gain a hearing, so she used her pseudonym in two ways: to emphasize the different roles of author and private person, and in consequence to enable her to be quietly outspoken as an observer and recorder of twentieth-century woman. Towards the end of her life she attempted to rectify what she saw as the exaggerated identification of her personal experience with the life and character of Alberta. Perhaps her most intimate writing is contained in the shorter forms of her art, in which she reveals herself both more immediately and obliquely than in the novel. The humour and pathos shown in the stories tally with the photographs[1] of her in early life, attractive, thoughtful, lively and laughing.

[1] Published in Jannikken Øverland, *Cora Sandel om seg selv* (Cora Sandel on Herself) (Den norske bokklubben, 1983). I am indebted to Øverland and to Gimnes, op. cit., for information regarding the dating of these stories.

The stories and reminiscences in the present volume are taken from the whole span of Sandel's work, from 'The Polar Bears' (1904) to the poem, 'Today the Rose', which we can regard as her final message, written as it was at the age of ninety-one in a form unusual for this author. Sandel was a prose poet and she builds up her descriptions with the careful eye of a painter. She is particularly conscious of light and its effect on the group of persons or objects illuminated by it: '. . . his hand entered the ring of light and joined company with the still life of fruit, flowers and golden reflections in the wine, grouped round an ice-bucket' ('The Bracelet'). This reminds one of the paintings by Louis Le Nain and Georges de La Tour which hang in the Louvre (which she must have seen), whereas her own paintings seem to be closer to Cézanne in colour and form. A literary parallel might be Virginia Woolf's description (written in the same decade as 'The Bracelet') of lamp-lit interiors in London in 'Street Haunting',[2] more particularly the unknown lady illuminated by the lamp as she pours tea in her Bloomsbury drawing-room. Woolf would certainly have subscribed to Sandel's aim to present 'the never-ceasing stream of life'[3] to her readers. But the sub-title 'Interior with Figures', which Sandel used more than once in her novels, could also be applied to many of the stories.

It is less easy to do justice in translation to the poet in Sandel. Her style pays equal attention to the sounds and rhythms of language, coupled with allusion, and these qualities cannot be conveyed unless chance similarities exist in English vocabulary and idiom. In particular she shares an awareness of silence typical of other twentieth-century Norwegian writers, together with the struggle to find precise meaning. 'Words are so useless. . . . But silence is heavy with meaning,' she comments in 'Avalanche'. In the same story the woman in distress is unable to find 'precise words that bring order to chaos and give relief', and her distress and confusion are thereby increased. When the description tends towards cliché – 'The old annual disappointments remain within her' – it is deflated by being contrasted with a startling image: 'like skewers in a piece of meat'.

The reader should bear in mind that the author's point of view is that of a Norwegian-born woman, growing up in a bourgeois home

[2] Included in *Death of the Moth and Other Essays* (Penguin Modern Classics, 1961), pp. 23–5.

[3] Øverland, op. cit., p. 213.

at the turn of the century (that important period in women's history), who became a permanent expatriate by leaving Norway for Paris to study painting; then accompanying her husband to Sweden, where she was to spend the rest of her life, returning to Norway only intermittently, though she kept in touch with her publisher and friends, and was awarded a Norwegian state stipend.

Such remarks as 'The summer is long in France. Anyone who owns the smallest patch of garden has plenty of time to spend in it' ('Puttycass') reflect the perspective of someone who has come from north of the Arctic Circle, where the brief period of long summer days is precious, and where summer warmth sometimes does not come at all. France, particularly Paris and Brittany, was a lasting influence and provides the background for much of Sandel's writing.

The sketches of animals, of cats in particular, reveal the personality of the writer, whether as owner or mere acquaintance. Her relationships were founded on respect, sympathy and trust, which were then returned by the strays which shared her family life. Wise information on how to treat animals is conveyed as well. But it is their characters we remember: 'He [Puttycass] possessed two priceless qualities to a high degree: humour and imagination.'

Above all she is concerned to record woman's experience, with sympathy, with irony. The woman in 'The Bracelet' thinks of herself as 'this unsuccessful, this abnormal and handicapped creature, a woman without a man'. The reactions of the people at the guest-house in 'Madame' are amusing on the surface, until we glimpse the tragedy of the displaced person, the woman who finds herself without purpose, rootless and lonely, as the result of a broken marriage, of living in different countries so that she has become a stranger in her own as well. In the words of the doctor who is consulted: 'When people are neither ill nor well and belong neither here nor there, it's not easy to know what to do about them.' And in the words of the narrator: 'Loneliness is a suggestive word that perhaps might have occurred to them, and caused them to fall silent.' Outwardly nothing dramatic happens to Maia ('Carmen and Maia'), but inwardly nothing will ever be the same for her again, after the moment when her boy-friend shows he is attracted to Carmen. He will not pursue Carmen, he may well marry Maia, but the first betrayal has destroyed trust.

Cora Sandel pays her readers the compliment of never underestimating their ability to pick up her hints. She never preaches, explains or expands on a point, simply nudges the mind in passing. In 'The Bracelet' we share the woman's disappointment when it is hinted that her lover's gift has belonged to his wife, and that she, like the bracelet, is being used at second-hand, to recreate what he has lost. But is that all? Has she not deceived him equally by being calculating about her relationship with him? Are they not equally at fault for deceiving one another? Or is Sandel asking for our sympathy for men and women disappointed in love, seeking a replacement, wounding one another in the very moment of hope? We do not know their names because we cannot predict their future. The wife – whom he has wronged by appropriating the bracelet which was a symbol of their love – has a name; she is of the past and the past is finished.

'There's a War On' also conveys its message with economy. There are no political comments, there is no moralizing; just a few hours of wartime experience focused on a three-week-old baby dying of hunger as it shelters from the bombardment of Paris in a cellar with its neighbours. When the baby at last begins to take the breast, there is 'a sound, a tiny sound of life itself', which asserts itself above the roar of the guns. 'Something is happening that is right and proper, something is beginning to grow as women think it should grow; nothing is being destroyed, something is being protected.'

'The Women at the Bath-house' is unusual in its setting in an unnamed African country at an undated point in time. It contrasts the superficially civilized, silk-clad life of the harem with the established traditions of a tribe, where a young girl can find more freedom, security and respect in selling her body to save a dowry for her future marriage.

Norwegian authors who lived through the years of the Second World War often produced at least one work expressing the trauma of the German Occupation, and Sandel was no exception. Sweden's contribution in providing a haven for Norwegian and Danish refugees from the Gestapo was significant. 'The Broad versus the Narrow Outlook' is her version of the rise of fascism in Europe as it affected the smaller European countries occupied by Nazi Germany. Ostensibly this is the account of the attempted take-over of a family's land in the country at the edge of a fjord, and the pressures put on adults and children, including the torturing of the little boys. The family's name, Olavsen, is as typical of Norway as Smith might be of

England, and Crown Prince Olav was the symbol of the Resistance movement. The mysterious, powerful leader behind the gradual acquisition of other people's land, Rudolf Heiler, with his forelock and small moustache, jackboots and peaked cap, is an easily recognizable Adolf Hitler. The children's names are barely disguised: Fritz, the ringleader, assisted by Hermann and Rudolf. The predatory adults encourage the children's cruelty by condoning their behaviour towards the peaceful Olavsen children, turning concepts such as truth and justice upside-down, and giving them the symbolic jackboots to wear, like those worn by their father and uncle. At one point Marie Olavsen exclaims, 'We're like a subjugated people.'

But it is perhaps in 'Avalanche', the description of an evening when a marriage breaks up, that Sandel's reticence is best conveyed. In spite of raised voices there are no violent scenes. The real drama is played out in the protagonists' minds, unspoken, rarely revealed, except to the reader. 'Fear seeps into her, woman's ancient fear of man, the master, who holds her fate in his hand.' But what about this liberation that is supposed to have come for the new woman? 'Only daughters with four children are not liberated,' she tells herself bitterly. But is he entirely in the wrong? She – they are given no names – suddenly glimpses 'the boy who never quite dies in a man, who always needs consideration, however old he may become'. At the last moment each has a desire to turn back, but their habit of silence makes the break irrevocable, and the devastation, the silence after disaster, is complete.

Like the artist she is, Sandel paints the picture for us, stands back, and says, 'Look!' It is to be hoped that many readers will accept her invitation.

Bergen, Norway Elizabeth Rokkan

The Polar Bears

I can hear them from my room. The first thing I hear in the morning is their hoarse, long-drawn-out roar ending in a tortured wheeze. In the evening it sounds through the dark, despairingly, filled with impotent anger and defiance – and now and again it rises to an enraged scream, followed by wild shouts from the boys.

They are shut in on the wharf below our house. They arrived a fortnight ago on the sailing-ship from the Arctic, and shortly they will be shipped out to some zoological garden.

I went down to look at them one day, picking my way between barrels of cod-liver oil, casks and bales of lumber.

It was noon. The walls were burning in the sun. There was a smell of spilt cod-liver oil, of ebb-tide and of dried fish. It was not easy to find what I was looking for. Crates, barrels, fish, lumber and sacks of flour everywhere. But no cage, nor anything else that might be expected to contain polar bears, was to be found. I thought I had gone the wrong way, and was about to turn back.

Then I suddenly heard a long sigh and the sound of a body turning over heavily. It seemed to come from one of the crates by the wall. I looked at them in astonishment. There were two of them standing beside each other, at the most a metre in length and breadth and at first glance lacking any opening whatsoever.

Then there was a movement again. Yes, it *must* be there. I went over and looked at the crate more closely. At the top of one of them was a crack between the planks, about the width of a finger. Through it could be glimpsed something shaggy and yellowish-white, moving slowly.

There really was a bear inside after all!

I tried looking through the crack at different places and finally managed to see the whole animal. It was a cub – how old, I could not decide; but at any rate it filled the length of the crate, and the height as well, as far as one could see. For the moment it was lying flat on its side with its limbs in front of it and its head stretched out, its eyes closed. Dishevelled, dirty, exhausted, it lay there on a layer of stinking straw.

I stood for a while watching it, and then there was a rustle in the crate next door. That one had no crack in the lid, and I had to go down on the ground in order to find a peep-hole. Yes, there was a bear in there too. It was sitting up, tearing angrily at a piece of dried fish. When it heard that there was somebody near the crate it turned its head towards the sound and looked about it, nasty and ready to fight. Its eyes were red and bloodshot, and it snarled softly.

It was used to being tormented. After a while it turned its attention to the fish once more, pulling and tearing at it, holding it steady with both forepaws.

Suddenly the fish was torn apart, and the bear's head thumped against the lid of the crate with a terrible thud.

It sat motionless for an instant as if to collect itself, then began pawing the straw furiously, while it cried in rage and desperation with its little black nose drawn back above its strong teeth. It continued crying and roaring for a long time. At intervals it drew breath with a gurgling sound and then started again with renewed strength.

But the bear in the crate alongside merely opened its eyes for a moment and then closed them again. Was his companion grumbling again? Hadn't he learned that all that rage was of no use whatever, that one could only give in, come what may? And it went on dozing, looking utterly resigned. Was it dreaming? Of cold, salt water, of the white polar wilderness, of the arctic night with its moon and its great stars?

Poor little polar bear! You will be taken farther and farther away from it. You will have to get used to more and more heat, and you will have to turn heavily in your stinking little crate for a long while yet.

And when you finally reach your destination you will perhaps be given a little pond to splash in. Oh yes, I expect you will, for we live in a humane age. A little pond, with lukewarm, muddy water and floating breadcrumbs from a well-meaning public.

By that time we must hope you will have forgotten the sea and the ice and the great stars of the arctic night.

The Silken Thread

The air in the studio is heavy and dry, as it usually is when you have had a model there for hours on end.

Rosina is telling me about the silkworm. She is sitting on the dais with her legs drawn up under her limbs, young and firm, but with something worn and slightly flabby about her body, as if she had been plump and had suddenly become thin. She is a warm golden colour, like a fruit matured by the sun. The narrow head with the tired face, aged too soon, is thrown back slightly; the brown eyes – usually veiled and turned inwards – are shining moistly. She draws her upper lip back over her white teeth in a broad smile, sweet and sad.

And suddenly one sees that Rosina must be telling the truth: that she is only twenty.

She hasn't told me much about herself. She hasn't the usual failings of a model: no upper-class family that she has broken with, no distinguished but strict father, who would kill her if he knew she was posing, and no mother who would die of shame. Nor is her father a childhood friend of President Poincaré, and she has not been educated in a convent among the daughters of the nobility.

And, the strangest thing of all: she hasn't taken me into her confidence about great artistic projects, about secret rehearsals, impending stage débuts or negotiations with impresarios at the Café de Globe.

All I know about Rosina is that she is from Asti and has spent three years in Paris and that she has the dogged tenacity of northern Italy in her work and the melancholy dreaminess of southern Italy in her eyes. Now she is lively and talkative all of a sudden on account of a silken thread that has attached itself to her. She twists the thread round her finger and stares at it. Then she holds it up in front of me and says, 'Silk's beautiful, isn't it?'

'Yes, it is, Rosina.'

'Strange to think that small animals make it.'

'Yes, Rosina. Have you ever seen silkworms?'

'Of course, signora! We had silkworms at home. We produced silk and sold it. Have you never seen how it's done, signora?'

'No. How is it done, Rosina?'

And so Rosina is set free on the path of candour, where we so easily gallop a little further than we would wish. It looks so innocent to begin with. One starts out so far from the great confidences. Even the most secretive of us are occasionally responsive to the little flick of the whip that chases us on. Rosina has been given it by the silken thread.

She tells me how the eggs are collected in the autumn and put under glass for the winter, and how in the spring they are carefully placed between pillows close to the warmth, how the whole house is warmed and how quickly and cautiously everyone moves about, so that no draughts will get in.

After a few days the pillows are teeming with tiny black larvae, each the size of a pinhead. If you offer them a mulberry leaf they will cling to it in their hundreds until it is completely covered, and in this way they are transferred to large wooden shelves, made specially for the purpose. There they sit eating and growing, eating and growing for twenty days. They eat at an incredible rate. Bundles of leaves are carried in to them, and only the little pithy skeleton remains, stripped neat and tidy.

Day by day they grow while you watch. When twenty days have passed they are long and thick as a finger and can no longer be transported on mulberry leaves, because they are too heavy. When they have to be taken to the long dried stalks where they are to sit and spin themselves into their own silk, they must be picked up with the fingers – and it takes courage to pick up the fat little beasts with your fingers.

One day they stop eating. Then they are placed on blocks of wood. And then the spinning begins.

'It's interesting, signora, it's exciting, believe me. You can't think of anything else as long as it's going on. You watch them all the time and talk about which one will be good and which one will not turn out well. You don't talk about anything else.

'And then comes the big day when they are taken carefully off the stalks they're sitting on and sent in baskets to the silk factory. Then the whole family is busy – everyone helps. It's like a party, signora. But you have to touch them lightly, you have to pick them off gently, so that they're not torn to pieces.

'Silk cocoons are beautiful, signora, like a delicate, brittle little eggshell of mother-of-pearl.

'But it's a busy time, as you can imagine, it makes work. And then there are the hens who have their chickens at the same time, and the guinea-pigs have their babies, and the rabbits.'

I sit wondering what can have driven Rosina away from all this, since it makes her voice warm and her face young to talk about it.

Then she says, 'And the bad cocoons were for me. I was allowed to sell them all on my own. I could earn eight to ten lire a time, if I kept my wits about me.'

'What did you do with the money, Rosina?'

The question slips out as so many questions do – any question, just for the sake of asking. What could a Rosina do with eight to ten lire a year?

'What did I do with it, signora? You'll never guess what I did with it.'

Rosina adopts a mysterious expression and puts a finger to her lips. She is no longer merely young, she is a child, mischievous and serious at the same time, as children can be. And she was beautiful as a child, maybe no more than three years ago.

'I hid the money, signora. I hid it under the roof thatch. I crept up when I was certain that no one was watching me, and I made a hollow in the thatch, to put the money in. One day there was more than fifty lire.

'I travelled with that money, signora.'

Rosina has become thoughtful. After a while she says, 'It's

strange, Mother was so kind to me that day. It was almost as if she suspected something.'

'Wasn't your mother always kind to you, Rosina?'

'No. She was strict, signora, too strict. She scolded me all the time. That's why I knew for many years that I would leave when I could. And one day I went to the station and took the train, and since then I've heard nothing from home. I wrote once from here, in Paris, but nobody answered. They're cross with me at home.

'Parents are foolish to scold their children all the time, signora.'

'Yes, Rosina.'

'I came first to Chambéry. That's just across the border. I got a place there as a housemaid. I've worked all the time, signora, I've always been honest. And later on I went to Grenoble, where I was in service with the justice of the peace. Oh, I had a good place in Grenoble. Everyone smiled at me, and everyone was kind, and I didn't have much to do. Mostly I answered the door when anyone rang the bell, and I wore little white aprons and a little white cap on my head, and everyone thought I was sweet – oh yes, signora, I was so young then.

'But the daughters of the house were beautiful, you know, and so kind, especially the eldest. When she got married I stood there the whole time and received the guests, and many of them gave me a tip. Oh, everybody was kind on that occasion, signora. And in the evening, when the newly-weds left, we all cried. Her mother cried and her father cried, and her brother cried and her sister, and I did too. But the bride didn't cry.'

'Was there a brother too?'

'Yes, of course, and he was kind too, too kind, signora. His mother didn't like it. Imagine, one evening he wanted to show me something in his room, and when we went through the salon we had to take our shoes off so that no one should hear us. And guess what, Madame turned up and saw us in our stockinged feet, both of us hand in hand. It was funny, signora. It was comical. But the next day I had to leave.'

'And then, Rosina?'

'Well, then I met my friend, my first friend . . .'

'Your first friend.'

'He had known me when I was with the justice of the peace, he had come to the house. He rented a room for me and bought me pretty clothes. But two weeks later he gave me money so I could travel to Paris. It didn't work out.'

'And then?'

'And then. Well, since then things have gone well,' says Rosina quickly, as if she thought it necessary to make that remark first. 'I've always had work. I've always been earning, except for the time I was in hospital. I've been a model all the time, signora, and I have my room and my own things. I'm alone when I'm there.

'I expect I'll go home one day, but not until I've saved a bit and can take a suitcase of pretty clothes with me. Then nobody will say anything, you see.'

'What was the matter with you when you were in hospital. Rosina?'

'Oh – 'Rosina looks down – 'things went wrong, you understand, in the fourth month, and then I became ill. . . .'

I make no comment and Rosina adds, 'What was I to do, signora? What would you expect? I couldn't bring a child into the world. What would I have done when I got fat and ugly and couldn't pose any more? What was I going to do afterwards? For I wouldn't have sent the child to an orphanage. . . .'

Her voice is raised and her face is flushed, and she gestures against me and against everything I am not saying but that she assumes I intend to say. 'Oh no, signora, no, no, no!'

'Are you well now, Rosina?'

'Oh no, I'm often in pain, signora. Something says tak-tak-tak inside my stomach when I walk fast and when I go up stairs. I often have to stand still because it hurts. At the hospital they say I won't get better without an operation. Sooner or later I'll have to let them do it.'

'Perhaps it would be best to do it sooner, Rosina, and get it over and done with.'

'Then I shall lose my friend, signora, I'll be sure to lose him if I'm lying ill in bed. We must not be ill, signora, the men don't like it. We have to pretend there's nothing the matter.'

There's no answer to that. It's true. It's risky for us to be ill, whether we are a prosperous bourgeois housewife or a little Rosina in an artists' quarter in Paris. Most of us know it, and we keep going as long as we can without giving up. It's our last halfpenny, in a manner of speaking. With it we can still achieve a little of all that our weakness needs: security and a little happiness – and peace and repose in two strong arms.

Alberta

Grandmama is ill – dangerously ill. It says so in the telegram that is lying open and spread out on the living-room table.

Mama is going to travel to Grandmama. She ought to have gone long ago, when Grandmama was taken ill, but it's such an expensive journey.

When the telegram arrived Papa said that of course – of *course* – Mama must go, wherever the money was going to come from. Of course she must just do her packing and get ready.

But the worst of it is, Mama ought to have gone long ago, and now she may get there too late, even though the boat is leaving in a couple of hours.

She goes up to pack, sniffling. Her eyes are red and her lips pressed tightly together. Every now and then she expels a long, deep sigh.

Papa has disappeared into his study. The atmosphere is stormy.

Alberta dithers around the suitcase, attempting to make herself useful and, if possible, to dissipate the storm. She doesn't know what to do with her cold hands, and wrings them as if freezing. With all her strength she exerts herself to appear sympathetic towards Mama, but her conscience is guilty, because all the time she is thinking about Papa in his study.

'Isn't there anything I can help you with?' She tries cautiously, since the last thing that happened was that Mama irritably took something which Alberta had brought her straight out of her hands and put it back on the table.

'No, thank you, my dear Alberta,' she said in that cold, bitter voice which Alberta dreads more than anything. 'You're only getting in my way. Leave me alone.'

Now Alberta knows very well that it will be wrong if she does leave her alone. Her palms are beginning to sweat. She moves out of Mama's way and keeps as quiet as possible.

Suddenly Mama, kneeling in front of the suitcase with her face bent over it, exclaims, 'And your father doesn't think of giving me a single little thing for the journey, Alberta. Never the least thoughtfulness – never the slightest little attention. I can't tell you how much it hurts me, now when I need to feel a little love about me. I feel so lonely, so lonely.'

Mama's voice is choked with sobs, and Alberta watches the tears roll slowly down over her cheekbones and disappear into the suitcase.

Then Mama puts in Grandmama's photograph.

'Like this picture of your grandmother, Alberta. It's been standing on the bedside table for years, getting faded and ugly and ruined, but it has never occurred to your father to give me a little frame for it. Only a small thing, of course, but. . . .'

Mama sniffs into the suitcase.

Alberta wrings her hands so that they risk being put out of joint. If her life were to depend on it, she would not know what to answer. When Mama calls Papa 'your father', it's like a warning bell.

Suddenly a door opens and someone calls 'Alberta!'

It's Papa.

When Alberta enters the study he is standing at his desk, holding a five-kroner piece in one hand. In the other is his open wallet. Alberta approaches him, her heart thumping.

'Look, Alberta,' says Papa, 'here's five kroner. Could you find some little thing for Mama that she might like to have on the journey? A small bottle of eau-de-Cologne, perhaps? I thought she might like it, and then I thought that now you're such a big girl, Alberta, you might go and buy it for Papa. I have so much to do, you know.'

Alberta catches her breath for relief and joy. *Could* she go and buy that little thing? Of course she could.

'Yes,' she says eagerly, 'of course I can. But I know of something that Mama wants much more than eau-de-Cologne, Papa.'

'What's that, Alberta?'

'She'd like a frame for Grandmama's picture,' exclaims Alberta, terrified lest she may not get it.

'Yes,' says Papa, 'but I'm sure she'd prefer some eau-de-Cologne for the journey. She can always have a frame some other time.'

'Oh no, Papa, no! I know she wants a frame. Nothing would please her more than a frame.'

'All right, all right,' says Papa. 'If you think so. Do as you think. That's the best thing, Alberta. I have so much work to do, as you see.'

Papa gestures at the desk and sits down. And he rubs his glasses before positioning them in front of his reddened eyes, which always look so tired.

Alberta reassures him yet again, 'Yes, Papa, yes', and hurries out.

After a while she returns from the hardware store on the corner with a piece of thick, polished glass which, with the help of a prop behind it, stands on two brass knobs. She has chosen it instead of all kinds of frames with metal scrolls and flourishes, and she feels certain she has chosen with good taste. She creeps on tiptoe through the kitchen and hall into Papa's study.

'Yes,' says Papa, looking at the object over his glasses, 'it's all right, but. . . . I must say I think it would have been better to get some eau-de-Cologne,' he adds. 'But take it in to Mama, then. You go in and give it her, Alberta. You can say it's from you children.'

Alberta goes out quietly and hangs up her coat. Then she goes in to Mama through the dining-room.

Mama looks up from the suitcase. The barometer is quite unmistakably pointing to storm.

'Ah, there you are. May I ask where you've been? Not one of you thinks of giving me any help, not even you, Alberta. I thought I could count on a little help from my big daughter, but I see I was mistaken. You all leave me alone to. . . .'

Mama's voice is lost in a sob.

'Mama,' says Alberta, feeling a choking sensation in her throat that makes it difficult to get the words out. 'Mama, I've been to buy this for you.'

'What is it?' says Mama, and her voice is so cold. Oh, Mama's cold voice. She takes the packet and unwraps the paper.

'Whatever is this? But, my dear Alberta. . . ?'

'It's, it's,' stammers Alberta, her composure already lost. 'It was Papa who – but then I said that I thought. . . . It's from us children. . . .'

She gets no further, for Mama interrupts her. 'What an extraordinary idea! If only he had bought a little eau-de-Cologne or something nice for the journey – the kind of thing other husbands think of when their wives travel.'

Mama's voice is like ice.

But inside Alberta something is jumping so oddly. Now she can feel that strange, painful pressure in her chest, as if her heart were turning over. And then will come the tears, that violent weeping that she cannot control. She knows it will. It's in her throat already, as she turns and runs out through the door.

Nothing irritates Mama more than Alberta's weeping.

And she rushes out and grabs the key to the only place where she can whimper and sob her heart out without embarrassing anyone.

Artist's Christmas

The daylight comes creeping in, stone grey, spreading slowly inside the studio, bringing out of the darkness, as if by magic, frozen windows, a cold stove, a dead world.

Both of them open their eyes simultaneously, each seeing the other's face at the same moment, the slightly haggard and sunken, dogged and tense expression that comes of cold, sleeplessness and inadequate nourishment. 'Come here and get warm,' he says softly.

Silently she moves in under his blanket. 'Christ!' he exclaims, when he feels how cold she is.

Shivering she curls up in the crook of his arm. A tear appears from under her eyelid, travels across her nose and falls heavily on his shirt-sleeve. 'There, there, there,' he murmurs. She gives in and cries helplessly, her face against his neck.

The water is frozen in the bucket, the ink in the ink-well. The panes in the windows and skylight are covered with frost patterns. He wanders about, noting it, while he buttons up his clothes and turns up his collar, trembling with cold. And he pauses in front of the still-life motif, where the flowers are hanging black and rotten and the leeks are lying like corpses. 'Look at this!' he calls out. 'All of it ruined. The jug's cracked from top to bottom. I shan't get anything more out of *that* picture.'

'We should have emptied it,' she remarks from the bed. 'We

should have thought of that when it got so much colder last night. The flowers wouldn't have survived anyway.'

'Oh, one always knows what should have been done when it's too late. Well, well . . . you stay there till the water's boiled for the tea.'

She curls up in the little patch of warmth left in the bed by their two bodies, listening to him hacking a hole in the ice in the bucket and tapping the bottom of the tea-caddy to find the last leaves. 'Good thing we've got some paraffin,' he mutters.

She lies with her eyes closed. She can think no further ahead than to tea, hot tea. The slight whisper of the flame reaches her like a reminder of a better world, a world fit to live in. When you listen to it and lie completely still so that none of the accumulated warmth escapes, it is almost cosy.

He is poking at the stove, raking out the ashes, blowing on his fingers and poking it again; unpleasant sounds that bother her. What's the use of making them today when they haven't so much as a shaving to kindle a fire with?

Then the sound of wood snapping. She half sits up in surprise. He is standing breaking a canvas frame in pieces against his knee. 'I'll light it as soon as you get up,' he says in explanation. 'Then you can get dressed over here by the stove. It's better than nothing.'

A warm wave of gratitude overwhelms her. A frame is no small sacrifice. 'Wonderful!' she cries in excitement. 'Then we'll have our tea in front of the stove.'

The tea warms so that it hurts the spine, the frame burns brightly. It lasts no longer than one might expect, just a few hectic minutes. Cup in hand they squat, turning their bodies so as to feel the warmth all over, greedily taking advantage of every last bit of heat from the embers and ashes. And then the chill is back again, making their faces pinched and grey.

On top of all her other clothes she is wearing his raincoat, over her stockings men's socks, and then wooden clogs. This uniform has come about of itself as the days have passed, cold and penniless. His clothes are ill-fitting and insufficient, the way clothes look when there is too much underneath them. He moves in them stiffly and laboriously.

The rotting floor is just high enough to leave room for the

rats; the studio is built virtually on the bare earth. In spring, summer and autumn it is an idyllic spot, the light falling on it attractively, ivy creeping in through cracks and openings. Artists and aesthetes are enraptured at the sight.

But then the winter comes. It turns mouldy and damp. The snow and the rain drip in, there are draughts from every direction, the stove with its crooked, dangerous tin chimney struggles vainly against it all. Sometimes it gives up and stands there cold and dead. Even the frost penetrates the walls and joins them indoors.

All in all one of those incredible dwellings, in fact condemned, which only artists and tramps can consider living in, and then only in Paris. Artists believe they can live anywhere as long as the rent is low and the lighting is good. They bribe the concierge and furtively move a couple of rickety iron bedsteads or a worn-out divan up to the attic. They have to live in misery for a long time before admitting to themselves and to others that they do so.

These two admit they are miserable. Things have reached that point. As recently as yesterday she made the beds and carried out the small daily rites that symbolize hearth and home, washing the dishes, dusting. Today she is doing nothing. With her hands thrust into her sleeves and her head down inside her coat collar, her eyes closed and her feet drawn up under her, she sits on his tall painting-stool, cowering like a sick bird.

He tramps around, now and again giving her a pat on the back in passing, before leaving her again. His attitude and expression are those of a malefactor. Their breath comes out of their mouths like smoke.

'You mustn't sit like this,' he says finally. 'It's dangerous. We must go out and take a brisk walk.'

'I haven't the energy. We walked all yesterday, we walked the day before yesterday.'

'Don't exaggerate. We sat for hours in the Louvre yesterday. We sat in St Germain des Prés as well. We're not the only ones to spend our time in churches and museums in this cold.'

She does not reply, merely crouching down farther. Her courage has vanished with the fire that has burnt out and died.

She coughs.

Then he takes her by the arm, forces her down from the stool, and says angrily, 'You'll be good enough to come this minute. They'll have to give us another day's credit at the corner. They can't let us perish. Here are your shoes.'

He helps her on with them roughly, with some exasperation. But he puts her feet under his vest while he sits on his haunches and blows into her shoes to warm them, then leads her across to the door. 'You keep the coat on.'

'Are you mad?' She is roused at once from her torpor, turns energetic, gets him to put on the coat, and they hurry out. The rent has been owing for a long time, and just as they are about to walk quickly and carelessly past the concierge, they are caught. A telegraph messenger is standing inside: the telegram is for them.

He signs for it with trembling hands and opens it. His pictures are on exhibition at home in Norway, and he has given that fact as a guarantee. The concierge watches him expectantly. The telegram says: A MERRY CHRISTMAS FROM ALL OF US.

He stuffs it in his pocket with a crooked little smile.

'Nothing of importance, monsieur?'

'Nothing of importance, madame.'

A biting wind drives them along the ice-packed pavement, carrying them with it as it carries paper, trash, withered leaves and other lifeless objects. They stumble in through the swing-door on the corner. The transition to the dense, stifling atmosphere indoors is so extreme that it is painful at first. It takes their breath away. Only gradually do they feel relief. And then it's all marvellous: the tobacco-smoke, the steaming coffee, the babble of voices, the clatter of coins and of checkers. Stifling, enclosed, unhealthy and marvellous. They are seized by a primitive need for shelter, a primeval longing to be together with other living beings, to share their warmth.

Only yesterday it had tortured her to see him pushing through the crowd at the counter, asking for credit yet again. Today she has only one thought: to be allowed to stay. Squashed into a corner at a small table, people coming and going all about her, the swing-door incessantly bringing in more frozen souls, she has only one idea: to defend her place to the death. When a steaming *café au lait* is put down in front of her she almost grasps the waiter's hand in gratitude.

They drink greedily and broodingly, reminding each other at intervals that they must not do so too fast. You can't sit for long over an empty cup on credit, not on a day like this. But immediately they are drinking again, unable to stop. They watch the colour rise, sudden and intense, in each other's faces, watch their eyes widen and shine. 'Better?' he asks. And he smiles.

He takes out the telegram. It's from her relatives. 'Did you remember that it was Christmas Eve?' he asks.

'Nobody forgets Christmas Eve,' she answers.

He puts his hand over hers. 'I'm going to find you something. We're going to have food and warmth before the evening, if I have to. . . .'

He doesn't finish. She says nothing. For a moment she waits, for the usual assurance that money *could* come in the course of the day, he could have sold something at home, the devil take them all if he hadn't. The assurance is not made. So he's thinking of begging again from his friends at the Dôme, going from table to table, explaining, giving assurances.

She draws her hand away and places it over his. 'Shall we try to manage one day more? On Christmas Eve the churches are open till midnight.'

He shakes his head obstinately.

Towards evening she is sitting squeezed into a corner of St Sulpice. The darkness is impenetrable beneath the vaulted roof. Lost in its infinity, powerless against its might, multitudes of tiny flames are flickering before the altars to the saints, all genuflecting in the same direction when shadows pass them and footsteps ring out coldly against the stone paving. Her ears are full of such ecclesiastical footsteps, she has listened to so many of them during the day, long able to distinguish the flat soles of the priests from those of other people, the young from the old, men from women.

She has no idea of the time. Vespers is over. Tall candles were lighted at the altar, pushing back a little of the darkness, modelling out of it rows of faces into warm, restless chiaroscuro. The scent of fresh incense cut into the old, stagnant smell, murmuring in Latin alternated with thin, urgent ringing of bells, the tiny, zealous silhouettes of the choirboys moved up and down the altar steps, coming, going, genuflecting. That must have been a long time ago.

He came in at some point, suddenly leaning over her in the dimness, a fragment of vanishing daylight from a high window falling on this tense face. She could see him only vaguely. Nevertheless it struck her that his expression was similar to that of the poor, a look of timid defiance, a slight twist to the mouth when he spoke. He had knocked in vain at more than one door. Nobody was at home, they were not even at the Dôme. God knows where they all were. This one and that one were said to have moved to a hotel, a hotel with central heating. Now he was going to try someone else. She would have to be patient a little longer.

He had managed to find a franc somewhere or other. They spent it on hot milk at a bar nearby, and chestnuts. It tasted good for a moment or two, but roused their hunger. And it was really uncomfortable to have to move about, stiff and sore as she was from sitting so long. She looked forward to curling up inside the church again.

He refused to give it up and stay with her. 'Hasn't it occurred to you that we haven't a roof over our heads tonight?' he said. 'We can't go home until we have something to build a fire with.'

Oh yes, it had occurred to her all right.

'And on Christmas Eve, too.'

'We must stop thinking about Christmas Eve. We're not children.' She swallowed something childish that was trying to surface through her throat in spite of everything.

'Go and sit down again inside.'

She cried a little as she watched him disappear into the dusk and the crowds, one of the many hurrying along to beg for the simplest necessities. It seemed to her that he had a new way of walking, a poor man's walk, his shoulders hunched up and his hands plunged deep into his pockets. He kept close to the walls of houses, walking in the way the homeless and penniless walk. She was so tired that she did not notice anything clearly any more, but this cut her to the heart. Surely we're not really poor? she thought.

She returned to the drowsy, incense-laden air of the church.

It is getting crowded, people are shuffling about, whispering, coughing. The cold light from a couple of electric lamps suddenly falls over the nave, chairs are being arranged; one or two old ladies, who have arrived in good time for midnight mass, find their places and doze. Working-class women arrive, burdened with little children clinging to their skirts or in their arms. They bring a gust of winter with them in their clothes. The smell of poverty mingles with the air of the church.

She stopped thinking long ago. But a sequence of isolated images is floating in a disorganized way through her brain, sometimes joining up into painfully clear visions: a bed ready for the night with flickering flames from a fire, a steaming soup-tureen, a hot bath.

The naïve authors of the telegram appear as distant and unreal as characters in a sentimental story; a little circle of people round a Christmas tree, the gleam of the candles reflected in their kind, ingenuous eyes. She can imagine them asking one another the perennial question, 'Shouldn't Gustav go in for something else? This painting. . . ? He doesn't sell any of it, does he?'

Supposing they came and asked her? Would she answer as she usually did, would she. . . ?

. . . Nobody cares about them, nobody notices them. They are just two pieces of flotsam, floating on a boundless darkness that is drawing them into the whirlpool and will suck them under. . . .

Far away on the beach are crowds of people. She catches sight of a childhood friend, an uncle, the sexton's wife at the place in the country where she used to stay as a child, the pharmacist over in the Rue des Plantes. All of them are dragging and carrying things, all of them are busy, all of them have somewhere to go. She calls to the pharmacist with all her might, 'We're drowning, we're drowning.' He hesitates. But she is only a piece of flotsam, and he goes away again . . .

. . . goes in through the school gate in the village at home. It leads to heaven. That's where they're all going.

. . . the assembly hall in the school at home, the vault of heaven bathed in light, scents and sounds streaming through it. They come from everywhere and nowhere. The air itself is ringing and singing, bringing light and warmth with it, for no source of light is visible . . .

. . . a garden . . . the garden at home . . . it's spring, she is picking flowers.

Suddenly she is sitting bolt upright and realizes that she has been asleep and dreaming. But the dream accompanies her into reality. Squeezed among crowds of people standing and sitting around her, she can still hear the air ringing and singing. The splendour of midnight mass is filling the church.

She looks round in confusion and finds a back she recognizes, a back in a raincoat and the face that goes with it. She can see it in half-profile, tilted upwards. All bitterness seems to have been smoothed away from it. It is young, calm, lost in untroubled listening, beautiful. It is like a reunion with the happiness they both shared before everything became so contentious and difficult. She stares at it in amazement. What is real, this, or the cold and darkness outside?

She feels strengthened and renewed. It was not heaven, but it was a moment's rest from the grimness of life. Someone is nudging her: a young working wife whispers, 'It helps to take a little nap now and again.'

As if prompted she looks down into her lap, at her hands. And now the dream continues, now she is dreaming that she is dreaming. Her hands are lying there and they are her hands, but a bunch of violets has been put into them. She stares at them for a while, then lifts them to her face. They *are* real, smelling at first only of moss and a damp cellar. And then of spring and of life.

He has managed a loan after all. And he is completely untroubled again. And he has bought violets for her because it is Christmas. That was kind of him.

She tugs at his coat. 'Thank you.'

He smiles down at her. 'Are you awake? Did you know you'd fallen asleep? You look like a different person. The mass has just begun.'

'How much did you get?'

He whispers the figure. He puts his finger to his lips. They must be quiet for the sake of all those sitting around them. With a triumphant expression he turns his back to her.

After a while she tugs at his coat a second time. She cannot stop worrying: 'We can never pay it back.'

'Pay it back? I've had a sale, silly-billy. At home in Haugesund. Met a fellow who's been looking for me all day. Gave me some of it in advance – hush. . . .'

Dumbly she leans back against the wall. After a while she starts singing: a hymn about Christmas and redemption.

It was no fortune. Three hundred kroner, if the truth must be told. But it meant food, warmth, a night in a hotel, at least one. Firewood, payment of the rent, a reprieve from poverty and ruin, new possibilities, new hopes. . . .

It is midnight. Crushed and pressed by the throng they are gradually pushed towards the exit, while the Christmas carols echo beneath the vaults and the bells in the tower reverberate through the roar of the organ.

The air streaming to meet them from outside is different from before. It is snowing. Thickly and softly and generously. There will be a thaw. The air tastes of childhood; it tastes of Norway.

The square is white. The fountain with its three enormous basins, each one inside the other, is etched in thick, fuzzy contours. Each black tree carries, and is united with, a white one. But the wheel-tracks in the street are already grey and wet. Here and there among the houses in the background the mist parts and light falls through it. The gleam from the arc lamps falls on to the square in large circles, giving it the air of a stage on which symbolic events are to be played out.

'What a motif!' Immediately he frames it all with his hands, moving them here and there to get the composition right, squinting through his eyes with his head on one side. 'What a motif! But I know someone who's going to have hot onion soup. And maybe turkey. And maybe wine. I know someone who's going to sleep at a hotel tonight and maybe tomorrow night. And pay the grocery bill and the café bill and the rent and the paint shop and buy firewood and tea and sole her shoes and . . . come along.'

They walk away quickly, arm in arm. Their bodies are springy and supple because they have money in their pockets and fresh credit. Because they can see the road ahead for just a little way.

'The still life,' he says. 'Damn me if I don't set up that still life again. I saw a jug exactly like it in Montparnasse yesterday.'

She feels like a traitor because just for an instant she permitted herself the thought that perhaps Gustav ought to go in for something else.

The Bracelet

She put down her spoon. And with the last piece of ice-cream biting cold against her palate and an increasing after-taste of vanilla in her throat, smiling, she took a cigarette from the open case that he was offering her across the table. Her wrist with the new bracelet encircling it moved for an instant into the light cast by the table lamp. Both of them looked at it, and then at each other. Her smile became more intimate, her eyes darkened.

'It's simply lovely,' she said.

'It's an antique,' he replied.

'I realize that. It's one of the most beautiful things I've ever seen. I can scarcely believe it's mine.'

'Oh!'

Embarrassed by the satisfaction her answer gave him, feeling it expressed in his face and unable to control it immediately, he turned, looking for the waiter and the coffee, and rapped on the table impatiently with his matchbox. Then he poured out the last of the wine into their glasses and raised his. 'Skål!'

'Skål!'

She was looking at him against the background of a balcony railing, a dark hedge and a patch of green autumn sky with one star in it. The little lamp shone on him softly and warmly from under its parchment shade. One arm was resting on the table so that his hand entered the ring of light and joined company with the still life of fruit, flowers and golden reflections in the wine, grouped round an ice-bucket. It appeared to her to be more distinguished than usual, almost refined. From the cigarette he was holding there rose a pliant, capricious plume of blue smoke that was drawing arabesques in the air.

He looked attractive at this moment; there was something about his appearance that she liked to see in men, something straightforwardly calm and matter-of-fact. Maybe she had missed it a little in him, found him a little – well, a shade too strenuously youthful.

Now he *was* young. The furrows round his mouth had disappeared and his forehead was smooth.

That's how he could be, that's how he was, when life treated him kindly. That's how he was going to be from now on. That's how she wanted him to be.

Through the murmur of voices and the continuous tinkle of china and cutlery came waves of music. They had to lean across the table in order to converse. For the most part they were silent, sitting listening to the snatches of melody, nodding in time to recognized phrases, looking at the people around them, exchanging glances about them, and smiling.

She felt a little light-headed. That was good. It made her numb, weightless, almost bodiless and unaccountable. Everything seemed to her now to be as it should be.

Was it frivolity? Far from it. Everything was right and proper. It was right and proper to be two, to come and go together with a man, to be looked after and protected again and receive presents, beautiful, valuable presents. She needed all this. She wasn't one of those free-and-easy women who can live alone.

The bracelet? Was there anything wrong with the bracelet? Couldn't he have given her something modern now that antiques are not being worn any more? That's the kind of thing men don't understand, not men of his type at any rate. She would see to it that she dropped a hint another time. An exquisite bracelet in itself, certainly expensive, gold and large topazes. He's not afraid of spending money. That's good. A comfortable feeling.

Has she been a little surprised, slightly shocked a couple of times because of things he said and did? Bagatelles, unimportant trifles! We all have different sides to our character; she did too. There he was, making her existence liveable and normal again, someone to be with. A handsome, youthful man, fun to go out with. It's not just that they have clung to each other like two castaways. She can feel a little more than merely grateful and warmly devoted to him and so on. This evening she knows it. Something is stirring in her sweetly and demandingly, something purely physical, as if waking and coming out of hibernation. Which is part of it, which ought to be there. Thank God, it's there now. She won't need to pretend that. . . .

Someone had to be the person who gave her moments like these, carefree moments of well-being: who rescued her from being short of money and from slavery to the office, two circumstances that do not suit her at all; from the unpleasant, embarrassing, almost naked feeling of being this unsuccessful, this abnormal and handicapped creature, a woman without a man; and from the wilderness in which she had found herself when the tumult and fuss of the divorce was over.

From the abysmal loneliness of the nights.

A rescuer *had* to turn up before too long. A rescuer came.

In a strange mood of mingled relief and anxiety, of sacrificial generosity and excited expectation and defiant frivolity, she had allowed herself to be rescued.

He was all that she needed most at that moment: head over heels in love with her. He said that before he met her he had been like flotsam adrift in the sea, alone, misunderstood, without illusions, without meaning to his life. Everything had been wrecked and trampled in a trivial and intolerable marriage. She had given him back his faith in what was noble and good in life, made him young again, and would and must be his. A bit old-fashioned and strange, but obvious, easily understood statements, that were heartening and made one feel like a woman and a person of significance again, not like a God-forsaken neuter.

And there he sits now, looking so handsome!

In a suddenly gay and sentimental mood she reaches out her hand to him across the table. And she experiences a piercing sense of joy when he leans over it and kisses it. She has a weakness for gestures like that. They give colour and glamour to life, a bit solemn and old-fashioned, but never mind.

'What are you thinking about?'

'About – about nothing in particular. About us two, I think.'

Yet again he is forced to turn his head to hide the satisfaction in his face. Her reply was so right. He manages to attract the attention of a passing waiter and orders a glass of water.

Then he has his face under control again and looks at her, gazing into her eyes significantly for a long time.

Privately he is thinking: That bracelet was successful. Lucky I had it in times like these. Risky? No. Amalie is in Rome, and will probably stay there. And Oslo's a big city. Would have been idiotic of me not to take it. Isn't she sitting there like a trustful little child, pleased with it and in love with me? Young and lively, a hell of a girl. *Too* young? Nonsense. Nonsense! Just as well things went as they did with Amalie and me, just as well I got her out in the end. About time too after twenty years of marriage, from the biological point of view. Simply the law of life. OK, she was generous about it and left her things behind, fine. I have to be able to offer something. And I must have someone. Free love and night life aren't for me, not in the long run. Expensive too. No – an adoring little girl who looks up to you blindly and uncritically – I've been lucky.

And he smiles at her. 'That's a nice tango they're playing.'

All of a sudden she notices his expression change, becoming anxious, slightly distorted, old. His hand too, lying on the table, becomes restless, searching for something to hold. At the same time he greets someone behind her in a reserved fashion. She catches him mumble 'Damn!'

'Who was that?'

'Don't turn round – not just now.'

'All right. Who is it?'

'Hush! If you must know, it's an old friend of – of my ex-wife. Her best friend.'

A friend? she thinks. A friend of. . . ?

She imagines someone grey and colourless who has existed and will go on existing somewhere. Someone a little elderly in flat heels and with a bun. One of these anomalies of nature who don't understand men, and who are no fun to be married to. Whom one feels partly sorry for and partly that it serves them right. An outsider.

He has scarcely mentioned Amalie, only talked about disagreements and totally different temperaments, implied that he has suffered a great deal. She considered it handsome and chivalrous of him, correct and fitting in every way. Amalie is a bore.

'Oh, do sit still, please!'

'Still? I am sitting still! I haven't once . . .

'You're waving that cigarette about so. Forgive me, I'm nervous, I . . .'

'*Waving* it about? I don't know what you mean. Where is she sitting? Has she just arrived?'

'This minute. Oh no, *do* sit still! Waving your arms like that.'

'What are you going on about?' she asks with irritation. She has not made one superfluous gesture, and knows it. It's not her nature, she is reserved and calm. He's actually treating her as if she had no manners. Is she not to be allowed to move every time an old friend of Amalie's appears? No, she does not intend to be as considerate as that.

But when she turned round she looked straight into the face of a woman who, with raised eyebrows and a slight smile, was sitting staring at . . . at her arm . . . at the bracelet?

A beautiful, elegant, youthful woman. Very beautiful. Did Amalie have friends like that? In that case Amalie too was perhaps. . . ? Tell me who your friends are and . . .

'Couldn't you have waited a bit before you turned round?'

'My dear, how should I be expected to know. . . ?'

The impression is carved in her brain, a combination of two raised eyebrows, a smile, the bracelet. And of the expression in two eyes. In one second it had changed from irony to – to sympathy?

To something like 'poor little thing'.

She feels an embarrassing flush rise in her face, and a distasteful thought enters her mind. Horrid thought. Something she had read the other day in a fashion article, that the last time it had been fashionable to wear antiques had been around 1910.

'You must excuse me,' she hears him say from the other side

of the table, 'but I've never been able to stand her.'

'Ask for the bill, will you please? I feel chilly, I'd like to go.'

He raps the table with the matchbox. 'Waiter!'

She really does feel chilly. Everything has changed, the evening sky behind the hedge is dark and dead. There is a draught from the veranda, the Venetian blinds are flapping. And the people around them have suddenly become so unpleasant. They are making senseless, stupid grimaces like figures in bad dreams, laughing false and forced laughter. Even the table lamp is giving out a cheap artificial light. Nothing is what it seemed.

Without looking to right or left, she precedes him quickly to the exit. Something she does not know how to cope with is lying like a paralysis in her mind. She is pursued by a sympathetic face, no, by two. Deep in her coat pocket she has twisted Amalie's cast-off bracelet from her wrist. It slaps against her leg as she walks.

'To hell with her for coming and spoiling the atmosphere for us.' His tone is hesitant, a little uncertain as to what she has understood and has not understood. A little hopeful as well. She can't have understood that. . . . He tries to slide his arm beneath hers.

She shakes him off and walks quickly ahead of him.

Carmen and Maia

Carmen turns up every weekday on the six o'clock train, and on the three o'clock on Saturdays. Carmen works in a factory or at a dressmaker's, probably in a factory. She is always accompanied by a pale, blonde friend whose only function is to get Carmen to talk, leaning her head against the back of the seat so that she stretches her long brown throat, blinks her feline eyes, laughs her low laughter; and to display her young mouth, red and open and full of sharp white teeth like a young animal. The friend's name is, as it happens, of no importance; she does not need one.

Carmen is small, slim, supple, with slender brown arms, bare to the shoulders. She has a small face with precise features, the same colour as her arms, framed in shoulder-length waves of dark, springy hair, which she swings and tosses in a carefree manner, knowing full well that it can lie and fall and fly as it likes, since it always does it attractively and in a way that suits her. She passes one of her thin brown hands through it like a comb, pushes it away from her forehead, and looks neat again. Or she will toss her head to get the same effect. Her temples are slightly hollow, only slightly, as if the hand of a sensitive artist had once gripped her across the skull and squeezed it, lightly and fleetingly, and a delicate little dent had remained in each of Carmen's temples.

The centre of Carmen's face is not beautiful. Her nose, it is true, is as curved and delicate as a dangerous bell, with perpetually trembling nostrils, but it is large. Her mouth is even larger, and puts over her strong teeth. It is not difficult to imagine Carmen as an old witch. For the time being she is a young sorceress. And enchanting rather than beautiful.

When she laughs you sit as if spellbound, staring at her mouth, this miracle of healthy blood and jawbone. Her canines are sharp and placed a little higher than the other teeth. It increases the impression of an animal's jaw. When she stops laughing the whole area round her mouth juts out too far. But her lips are large enough to cover it, revealing long, curved, sinister corners. Her expression is as changeable as a cat's. It is calm, open and straightforward, or it hides itself under the curve of her forehead, blinking brown and blue. It can also have something mute, impervious and pitiless about it, that brings death sentences to mind.

But then Carmen can also sit chatting with her friend with an ordinary, kind, good expression, and even with a piece of crochet in her hands. Carmen is like the wind and the weather, never the same for long, and perhaps never quite the same as at any time before.

It is summer now, and she wears alternately two very simple muslin dresses; both have a small pattern in black and white. They fit her slender body as if they had grown from it.

Heaven alone knows what she has on underneath. It can't be much. On her legs are thin, coffee-coloured stockings and flat shoes in the same colour. She sits swinging them idly, balanced on the tips of her toes, lets them drop to the floor, then sticks her feet into them again, thoughtlessly and carelessly. Over her shoulders she has an old trench coat the colour of burnt tinder, like desert sand. She hangs it up in the corner behind her, and leans her head against it when she laughs. Round her neck a thin gold chain, round her wrist a tiny little watch. And nothing on her head.

Nothing on her face either, neither powder nor rouge.

Carmen is one of the chosen ones who can throw on an old sack and look just the same. Carmen has no need to beautify herself. She is brown, a pale unchanging brown that comes from within and has nothing to do with sun-tan or sun-lamps. She is slim and supple, young, enchanting rather than beautiful; hard when she feels like it, and affectionate when she feels like it, and with her hair just as pretty even if you were to turn her upside-down. And she knows that this is sufficient.

Carmen is a throwback from a dark, strange race, mingled once upon a time with our light Nordic blood, and produced anew. Her colour sense is sober and classic, and she does not abandon it for a garish summer fashion, does not allow herself to be tempted by dissipated flowery or striped material. If Carmen had been a lady she would probably have worn black, perhaps with a pearl in the lobe of her ear. But Carmen is only a factory girl.

When she walks through the railway carriage, lissom and light as if dancing, with the old trench coat slung over her shoulders, when she sits down in her corner and lets you hear her low laughter for a moment – oh, then the bold, painted summer girls in red and blue haven't a chance, even though they sit as seductively as they can, one leg slung over the other and an elbow on the window-ledge, pretending to be absorbed in a book. Every male looks up from his seat and listens as if to a decoy calling in the forest. Their faces boyish and confused, they sit turning their heads towards Carmen, not even pretending indifference. They look almost a little frightened. And when she has arrived at her station and leaves the train, they cannot control themselves, but lean out of the window craning their necks, while she prances past them carelessly on the platform below.

She does not even see them. She accompanies the same friend, and has no need to hang out her snare all the time on the train and elsewhere as many must. Carmen knows that if she really wants someone she'll get him. As if drawn by a magnet he will come to her and become hers in the fullness of time. Until one day, perhaps, when she will turn on her heel and prance away. Carmen knows her power, a knowledge that does not diminish it. And perhaps she has long since achieved her heart's desire.

Whereas poor Maia . . .

Well, to start with nobody feels at all sorry for Maia. She has what many in the compartment set out to get, a sweetheart. A boy of the skinny, weather-beaten, toothless-too-early type, with kind, beautiful, trustworthy eyes. They light up as soon as he looks at Maia, with all the gratitude a boy can feel towards the girl who gives him what his youth demands. Every pay-day he buys Maia something pretty. He leans forward, elbows on knees, and looks up at her, wearing the pretty object, unable to take his eyes off her as they chat together.

They are on the five o'clock train on Saturday, pay-day. The day when Maia, who is without any doubt in service, is free for the afternoon, and travels in to meet him when he comes from work, his clothes and face oily and dirty, his kind, beautiful eyes glowing through the grime. Since the spring they have made a variety of purchases which now adorn Maia's person. Gradually she has acquired a hat, a coat, a dress, handbag, sandals, all in different shades of red. Maia is in red right down to her feet, which hurt her in the new sandals. At any rate she often exclaims 'Oh! My feet!' and, when there is room, puts them up on the seat opposite.

Maia's face is red too. Red, a little plump and a little pimply, with a slack red mouth in the middle. When she removes her red gloves, her hands are also red and a little swollen from dish-washing and more dish-washing, floor-washing and clothes washing. The only thing about Maia that is not red is her hair, which, peasant yellow, unevenly and badly cut, sticks out from under her hat. And her eyes. They are pale blue, open and round, without a trace of feline mystery. You can look right through them and to the bottom of Maia immediately.

Sometimes the pair of them take a later train because they have been to the pictures. They sit and gaze at one another sleepily, squeezing each other's hands, enjoying each other's company. Perhaps Maia will take off her hat and enjoy a short nap between stations with her head on her sweetheart's shoulder, and with her swollen feet that threaten to burst the straps of her sandals up on the opposite seat.

Everything went its accustomed way for months. Carmen, mysterious and fascinating, swayed on and off her three o'clock and six o'clock trains. Maia and her sweetheart went shopping together in town and went to the pictures. They took the five o'clock and the nine-thirty trains.

But one day the devil felt like amusing himself, so he took the contents of the trains and shook them up. That seems to be the simplest explanation. Carmen made her entrance, swaying as if dancing the habanera, her trench coat over her shoulders and her friend in tow, normal in every detail, but on a five o'clock train. No parcels in her hands, nothing to indicate that she had any errands. She simply arrived.

Maia and her sweetheart were sitting as they usually did, holding hands and relaxed, their backs to Carmen whom they did not see. Until a couple of stations later, when Carmen leaned back and laughed at something her friend was saying. Then Maia's sweetheart turned his head instinctively, as if to a decoy call, and there sat Carmen with her long brown throat and young open mouth, blinking her eyes, while pearls of laughter rolled out of her, low, shapely and melodious.

It is true that Maia's sweetheart turned back to Maia and listened to what she was saying, but distractedly, with half an ear. Shortly afterwards he turned again automatically and looked at Carmen a second time. And after that he gave the wrong answer to something or other.

An instinct, an inner voice, must have told Maia that it was now time for her to look round as well. She stuck her red face with the peasant yellow tufts of hair beneath her red hat over the back of the seat and looked straight at Carmen with her pale blue eyes.

And Carmen stopped laughing. Her mouth closed, and long, sinister creases appeared in the corners. Her expression turned mute and pitiless beneath her curved forehead. Maia's round eyes stared for an instant into those of the sphinx and came back even rounder than before. They sought for and found those of her sweetheart. But her sweetheart's were distant and a little helpless, and Maia found no explanation in them.

The conversation started up again, but it was far from being the same as before. When one of the participants is absent, and turns his head for the third time, as if drawn by a string, it is not easy either. And now Carmen assumed a deliberate role in the drama.

She did not change her expression. But something happened to her eyes. Something passed through them, reminding one somewhat of a cat with cream. It is scarcely probable that it was for the sake of this dirty, oily boy with the slightly sunken cheeks. There was at any rate no lack of men with handsome eyes and not a trace of oil or dirt about them who craned their necks after Carmen. So it is more likely that it was because of Maia, because of Maia's pale blue eyes as they rose, quite stupid with astonishment, above the back of the seat.

So, for whatever the reason, Carmen allowed her expression to attract attention just then: nothing significant, just a lazy shadow passing across it. When Maia's sweetheart turned back to her for the third time, Carmen smiled to herself, briefly, almost unnoticeably. And resumed her conversation with her friend.

But Maia's sweetheart gave Maia nonsensical answers. He went so far as not to answer her at all, but merely sat in thought twisting his cap and staring out of the window.

Maia, however, took up the challenge, clumsily and pointlessly. She was far from realizing that Carmen was out of the ordinary, but she felt that something had to be done. She started to fence, desperately and wildly, holding out her wrist and remarking, 'Ought to have seen to my watch too. It's going wrong again.'

'All right,' he said, absent-mindedly and incorrectly.

'Can always get Christian to take it in on Monday. Expect I'll meet him tomorrow,' said Maia, playing for high stakes out of her own ignorance.

'Oh yes, of course,' exclaimed her sweetheart, even more incorrectly, quite hopelessly impossible.

'Christian'll pay for it for me, if I ask him.'

'Expect he will.'

Oh, men! They never understand their own good before it's too late. Suddenly Maia starts to cry, and hurriedly takes out her handkerchief. Maia's tears, clear and round, start rolling down her chubby face. Only with difficulty does she keep back her sobs.

'But what on earth. . . ? But Maia?' Her sweetheart understands nothing. He had been far away, nice boy though he was. He had not even reacted to the idea of Christian being the one to take the watch to town, he had not reacted to anything at all. 'What were we talking about?' he asks helplessly. And he miraculously remembers, and honestly wishes to make amends.

'You know I'll pay for it. I didn't mean it like that. I was just sitting and . . . and thinking about something . . . I. . . .'

And he believes this will make matters better, but no, far from it. Maia hiccups a few words into her handkerchief. He has to lean very close to her and ask her several times before he understands what the matter is.

And it is the ancient complaint, a thousand years old: 'You don't care for me any more,' Maia must have said, in the far-sightedness of misery, for he assures her unhappily, 'Ever heard of such a thing, Maia! Well, I never! How can you say such things?'

He is not nearly so far-sighted as silly Maia. He feels he is without guilt, and very unjustly treated, the more so when Maia pushes him away and continues to cry on her own.

So he is left sitting there, elbows on knees, twisting his cap. Everything has become embarrassing. After a while he puts a hand on his thigh, adopts a manly and independent pose, and looks out of the window as if considering serious matters.

Beside him Maia has finished crying. More puffy and red in the face than ever, she too looks out of the window with vacant gaze. Once she makes some remark in a low voice. He replies coldly, not looking at her, and goes on twisting his cap. He is offended and shows it, since in his judgement he has every reason to be.

Unnoticed, he glances at her quickly. There she sits, tear-stained and ugly. And when women start looking like that, without a trace of a reason, but out of sheer cussedness, pure and simple, no thanks! That's when you know what time of day it is. He had thought everything was fine and dandy between him and Maia. Yes, thank you very much! Better than anyone else? Of course she isn't.

Suddenly he turns round, as if pulled by a string. Pearls of quiet laughter are rolling out of Carmen's corner. . . .

Carmen wins. Carmen always wins. She is enchanting rather than beautiful, affectionate when she feels like it, and pitiless when she feels like it. She is sovereign in Cupid's realm.

She is adventure, risk, incitement, capriciousness, everything that eternally spellbinds young and old boys' minds.

Whereas poor Maia. . . .

The warmth that smoulders in everything and everyone can certainly catch fire and burn clearly and brightly and Saturday-cosily for Maia. But if Carmen comes by and only so much as blows on it, it will flicker at once, ready to catch fire elsewhere.

Perhaps Maia will never get it to burn quite so cosily on Saturdays again.

After all, she really is very clumsy at handling fire.

Simple Memories

Brémoder, 1916

A naked, open stretch of coast, the most unproductive and the poorest in Brittany, perhaps in France.

Above it in good weather and an offshore breeze the clouds pass like an endless procession of giant quilts, piled the one on top of the other, throwing shadows on to the gentle slopes, where sparse, short grass grows in the sandy soil. Then sudden strong currents of scent will arrive from richer areas, from lush summer landscapes far inland. But mostly they smell of the sea, seaweed and sea-wrack.

The ocean confronts it. The solitary trees tempting fate here and there beside the bed of a stream arch their backs against it, all their branches and leaves bristling landwards. The hiss of the surf is unceasing.

For mile upon mile the coast is fringed by shining white beaches. In good visibility it can be seen from Pointe du Raz in the north to Penmarch in the south, where the lighthouse stands. Scarcely visible in the daytime, at night two huge wings of light revolve from it. As quick and as regular as heartbeats they accompany each other over the surface of the sea and the tilting land.

Small clusters of human habitation are scattered on the slopes, all of them exactly the same. Broad, low little cottages, the walls roughly built of boulders taken from the soil. They turn their backs to the land; there are no doors or windows that side. But towards the sea are whitewashed façades, light blue doors and window-frames, and a wide surround of hewn stone round all the openings and on the corners. They look that way. Some of them have small attics, and all of them have three rooms in a row, two for the humans and one for the animals.

Behind the tiny window-panes stand geraniums, crowded and luxuriant. And along the house wall, if there is a little prosperity and not too many children, and someone who has the time to think of such things, grow dahlias, the flower of all small coastal gardens. But usually there are too many children, and a pig left loose to root it all up.

Small houses, sprung up on poor soil, only as high as could be permitted in the face of wind and weather. They are clustered together for company and protection, and from the clusters stone walls trail across the slopes like the web around a spider, enclosing small potato patches, small barren fields, small grazing areas where white clover and bird's-foot trefoil sway in the wind; and cabbage patches, green as verdigris.

On roofs and walls yellow lichen grows plentifully. The people are dressed in black, the women wear a headdress of white, stiffened tulle. Grey, white, blue, black, yellow and innumerable shades of green: those are the colours of Brémoder.

It has looked exactly like this for a long time. The surrounds of hewn stone and the small mansard windows that are still fashionable are modest descendants of castle decoration in a grander century. They succeeded a style of building that had its roots in the Middle Ages, and that framed doors and windows in Gothic arches. Things are tested thoroughly here before changes take place. For this reason the French authorities fight a vain battle in many ways in Brémoder.

The moisture from the sea speedily bestows its patina, as always. The old and the new look almost the same. What provides distinction is the date carved above the door, together with the name of the first owner and of his wife. 'Jean and Catherine' it may read. Or 'Marie, widow of Joseph'; for Joseph is the head of the household, even when he is dead, now as in former times.

The earth provides, enough for people to fatten one pig a

year and keep a cow alive. The ocean provides the rest. It is their fate, their only hope; they submit to it and seek protection against it from the Virgin Mary and St Anne. The ocean is what makes rich and poor, here as along all coasts the world over. For the most part poor. Sardine and crab fishing, kelp burning, the methods simple and ancient, all of it a lottery. One would have to go far to find a horse. Yet life is lived here too.

The husbands go out to fish. The wives look after hearth and home in the manner of mothers and give birth to child after child in the big box bed. They help one another with the patch of earth and the kelp, wresting the annual cow-fodder and pig-feed from the meagre soil with the same primitive implements and the same drudgery as generations before them have done. And the bread, the basis of everything.

In centuries-old companionship the children and the pig and the chickens go in and out across the threshold. And inside the cottage objects stand as they are supposed to stand and as they have always stood, as long as anyone can remember with certainty. First the large cupboard, then the small one, then the wall clock, then the box bed, all of them richly carved.

In the small cupboard the bread is kept, large round loaves, treated with respect as befits their value. Above it stand rows of plates, and on the cupboard mementoes are arranged as they came into the house: the photograph, hand in hand on their wedding day; other photographs, taken by travelling photographers at different stages of the children's lives; shells and curios from expeditions while they were on military service. Above it all hang the pictures of *Our Lady of the Shipwrecked* and *Our Lady of Safe Voyages*; and small embroidered prayer samplers to them: 'Our Lady of the shipwrecked, protect us'; 'Our Lady of safe voyages, hold thy hand over us, for the ocean is wide and our boat is small.'

The young son goes fishing with his father. He is as slow and strong as a bear and as alarming as a force of nature. He wears his cap tilted over his eyes, throws stones and spits a long way, and is a danger to man and beast. He comes back from his four years in the navy with his cap on the back of his neck, brisk and lively, with forelock and square blue collar, a danger to female hearts. He marries, is given the one room in the family house, and goes out fishing again. In a few years he has acquired what he ought to acquire: his own house and a little land, a pig and many children. And the wheel turns once more.

Life is monotonous and harsh, the people somewhat dulled. The ocean has left its mark on them as it leaves its mark on its own everywhere. They know the anxieties of stormy nights, they know the moods of the sea and of fate. Yet they have their hidden humour, are always ready to venture out, their rituals of happiness and celebration traditional like everything else out here. For centuries their clogs have thundered across the earthen floors in the gavotte, the bagpipes have chirped like crickets at weddings, folk-song has been part of daily life. And folk-song in Brittany is history, going back to the oldest Christian times and further:

> Daik, mab gwenn Drouiz; ore;
> Daik petra fel d'id-de
> Petra gannin-me d'id-de.*

But now more than two years have passed since anyone danced at Brémoder, and the bagpipes are silent. When the young girls go to mass they no longer put the lace bib, the masterpiece that was their pride, at their breast, but a piece of black crêpe instead. They no longer walk in long lines in the evening and sing; they do not sing at their work, nor when they are driving the cows. Only the grinding of the loads of kelp, struggling up from the beach through the deep sandy soil, can be heard, the clatter of clogs on the rough roads, the wet slapping from the washing-place at the stream. And the piteous squealing of the pigs wherever they are being slaughtered on the farms.

It is no longer fitting to sing, or to play music, or to wear a white bib. It is fitting to speak quietly, to behave a little cautiously. One no longer knows what loss may have just struck the person one meets.

The day it happened was an agitated day at Brémoder. Some

* Listen, thou gifted pupil of the Druid; / Answer me; listen, / What shall I sing for you?

people gathered and marched to the priest's house in Plouhinec, stormed into the courtyard and accused the priest of being responsible. He ought to have been on sufficiently good terms with the Almighty, seeing that he was a priest, so as to prevent such things happening. The most unruly elements broke a couple of panes of glass.

But the parish priest of Plouhinec is a man of authority, tall, fat and venerable. He was at no loss for an answer. Had he not been obliged for years to admonish certain persons by name from the pulpit on Sundays, with every reason to do so? Had they not been more than legitimately drunk many times and caused uproar? Had they not been quarrelling, man and wife, and given a bad example? Had they not in their youth and frivolity set themselves above spiritual and temporal ordinances, forgotten their childhood teaching, brought illegitimate children into the world? Had they not spread slander about one another and neglected to attend mass? There had been much for which to criticize them down the years. The Almighty could hardly be blamed for finally losing patience.

The most wilful and hardened of them shouted that they had never been so sinful as to deserve this. It was the priest who did not understand how to deal with the Almighty.

'This was deserved, and more,' answered the priest.

A few more stones were hurled at the window-panes. But then the lawful authority arrived, from Pont-Croix and from Audierne, in full strength on horseback and on foot, and dispersed the crowd. The next day there were only women and children and old people left in Brémoder.

The old men had retired. They sat outside their cottage doors, keeping an eye on the pig and the weather, busy with their whittling and their nets. They had been fishing for forty years and had a state pension, and usually four or five sons to depend on as well. The stool in the chimney-corner was theirs. Here they could sit and ramble in the manner of old folks, remembering the war of 1870; but it was at the same time too distant and too close and interested nobody very much.

Now they had to turn out again, working in the fields and on the beach and up to their knees in the sea, gathering the kelp as they had done many years ago; they were forced to go out in the boats with the young boys, so that at least there was enough of a catch to cook fish for dinner. The small fields still produced their corn, the potatoes gave what they should, the kelp was collected and burned and delivered at the right time in the right amount to the factory in Audierne, the next year and the next. The women and children and old men did their best, and so life went on.

The oldest of them grew up at a time when nobody learned to read. For many years they managed perfectly with oral transmission where both the past and the present were concerned. But since this happened they have been gathering in the evening to listen to someone reading the newspaper. Only the men, naturally.

This takes place in a cottage up the hillside. A fourteen-year-old boy does the reading. He could have been relieved, for when permission was given a while ago for fathers of six children to be excused war service, a number of people with book learning came home. But by that time he had become an institution.

With a candle in front of him and the newspaper spread out on the table he sits, cramped and uncomfortable, in the crowded little room, tracing the lines with his finger. The air is heavy and thick with tobacco, wet clothes and human warmth. It is as if cotton wool were impeding the young voice that works its way monotonously through *Le Nouvelliste*, the highly ecclesiastical, the only newspaper that reaches us here.

Now and again a clog scrapes the floor, and someone spits with deliberation. But not much is said. Was it bad luck, like fire and shipwreck? Not much can be said about such things.

From time to time one of those who have been 'over there' may turn up: a soldier on leave, a father of six, or one of the injured who is no longer useful. Then the faces turn towards him repeatedly as if to discover what weight to attach to this news from the battlefield, written elsewhere with the blood of their sons, and brought to them through the mouth of a child. Not an eloquent child either.

But on Saturday evening they are all in one place, according to old custom. It is the evening when, in normal times, the share of the week's fishing was dealt out. Then tongues are loosened, and the hidden strategist is revealed. Then a buzz of talk rises from the cottage.

The women, young and old, carry on as usual, going up and down to the shore, to and fro between the house and the potato patch. They carry the basket of kelp or of cabbage for the cows on their heads, thus acquiring their singularly tranquil, dignified carriage. They meet and pause and exchange a few words. Somewhere a faded military cape, patched and washed, may be hanging out to dry over a fence. It is noted and commented on. A man is home for a few days. That's good to know. But he'll have to leave again soon.

Or they invite each other indoors and have something to show; something that has already found its permanent place among the curios in the living-room, as is fitting. But they are often weighed in the hand, shown often: cartridge cases, large and small, finely polished and decorated, ingeniously turned into flower-vases, tinder-boxes, penholders, needle-cases, objects of great weight and significance; the refuge of a man during insufferable hours and days, a sign that he was alive at that moment at any rate, that he is holding out and thinking of what he should be thinking – the people at home.

And now the parish priest admonishes them no longer. He has no reason to. The people at Brémoder have become docile. The young sinners are away at the war, and the sinning girls have nobody to sin with. They are kneeling before lighted candles. Never before have so many of them burned before Our Lady and Jeanne d'Arc and St Anne. Early mass is never skipped, and on Sunday the church is full of white headdresses. They resemble a flock of birds that take flight and settle again, when they genuflect. But the big black mourning bonnets are like ravens among them. With every week that passes there are more of them.

Some of the wives look more confident than the others. They are the ones who have six children or are carrying the sixth.

And some of them are taut round the mouth and pale inside the black bonnet. They are the ones who have received one of the official documents which are inscribed *He gave his life for his country*.

Two figures are coming up the slope from the sea, a woman and a dog. The woman is thin and slightly bent, flat and angular in outline. She keeps her hands hidden under her apron as modesty demands, and her arms jut out like two curved handles on her person. She is hurrying, pigeon-toed in her clogs, as if her life depended on it.

The dog is small, short-legged, of indeterminate breed, thoroughly unkempt. It runs on ahead, stops and looks back, then runs on again.

They are Tintidil and Petit.

And there *is* something of concern. When still at a distance Tintidil takes something white and square from her bosom and waves it. So we know what has happened. The letter has arrived, one of the letters that Tintidil starts waiting for as soon as the last one has reached her; tangible proof that there are still people who are related to her.

In a short while she is standing in the kitchen with Petit.

Close to she is all skin and bone; sinewy, tanned and wrinkled, hollow-chested and hunchbacked, as toil and poverty and rough weather can make a woman. Beneath her broad cheekbones and round her large mouth with the protruding teeth all plumpness has disappeared a long time ago. Her head is not unlike certain preserved heads of savage tribes that one sees in museums. But her eyes are as alert and guileless as Petit's, and no smile is warmer than Tintidil's smile, grotesque as it is with those large, protruding teeth.

The letter is either from Yser or from Corfu, from Pierre or from Jean. On the outside is written *Widow Stéphan.*

It is read aloud and interpreted by Marie-Catherine, our guardian angel, who is the literate member of Tintidil's circle. Tintidil herself cannot speak French, nor can she read or write. That kind of knowledge is a male prerogative in Brémoder. A man does his military service, and that is when he learns it. Obligatory schooling is merely nominal. The people of Brémoder are anything but law-abiding.

The letter is just as it should be.

First come the lengthy wishes, used by generations, ready-made once and for all, that the letter may find the addressee in the same good health as the letter-writer, God be thanked, enjoys. It has been worded thus in the letters from men doing military service, and from men far away at sea during all the years of peace, and the war has not changed such expressions. It has merely given them increased importance. On the day when something has changed it will be because disaster has struck.

Then follows the news. Brief little messages about comrades, about the weather, about parcels and letters that have arrived. And then the closing lines: 'There is nothing more to write about this time, but I embrace you, dear Mother, with all my heart. Your son who loves you.'

Marie-Catherine reads with the unctuousness that a certain minimum of book learning bestows, a feeling of solemnity at being able to read that has not quite been overcome. The difficult sentences, learned by rote, become in her mouth the important messages they really are. Nothing is lost, neither what is written in the lines nor between them.

Tintidil listens with her hands in her lap and her mouth open, like a child listening to a fairy story. Her eyes never leave Marie-Catherine's lips. Afterwards the letter is passed from hand to hand. All of us are allowed to hold it and read it, and Tintidil observes carefully the effect it has on each one of us. Then she folds it up and hides it in her bosom again.

'That's good news, Tintidil.'

'Yes,' says Tintidil. 'Good!' And she nods many times. She has a strange little patch of red on each cheekbone and is smiling her wide smile.

In the evening she visits Marie-Catherine again.

She sits with her hands under the table like an obedient schoolgirl. In the middle of the table is a candle. And on the opposite side Marie-Catherine is writing in the sweat of her brow to Tintidil's dictation. It is not going smoothly, for someone who cannot write herself has great difficulty shaping her thoughts. But finally it is all written down, more or less as intended. First the wishes for good health, then news of events. The pig has been slaughtered, the potatoes lifted, the kelp burned and sold. And then comes the moment when Tintidil, longing to put something more in the letter, something extra nice and amusing, something intimate and affectionate perhaps, who knows, leans forward and says to Marie-Catherine, 'Think of something, do think of something!'

For Marie-Catherine is one of the initiated, one of the great fellowship who hold the keys to wisdom. She must know the formula for what is moving so foggily in Tintidil's brain and heart.

Her name is Dil or Delle. Tinti means auntie. When a woman reaches old age in Brémoder everyone calls her Tinti. It grows on to her name: Tintidil. She is never called anything else any more, except in the registers of the *mairie* and on the outside of letters.

She lives in the smallest and loneliest of all the small houses, the one nearest the sea. Until a few years ago she lived a little way inland. But then the sea began to eat away the sandbank on which the house stands, a piece of it every winter. Now it is so close that it dashes against the walls at every high tide and swell. Then the sea spray darkens the panes and the little cottage takes in water like a boat.

A long time ago people began saying that they wouldn't want to be in Tintidil's shoes. On the worst of the stormy nights she moves out to her nearest neighbour, with Petit and the cat, the pig and the five chickens; and with the possibility in view of being without a roof over her head when morning dawns.

Indoors the house is reminiscent of a ship's cabin at sea. The two box beds with their red curtains and quilts look like genuine bunks, and the large cupboard, the small cupboard and the wall clock all adopt a threatening tilt in the same direction, owing to the unevenness of the earthen floor. Through the tiny window comes just as much light as into a proper cabin.

The curios are in their place and mark the phases of Tintidil's life. There is the big shell from when Jean was in Cochin-China, and the rush fan from when Pierre was there. There is the extraordinary bottle with a three-master under full sail inside it from Stéphan's years at sea, and there is

Stéphan's watch. It still stands at the exact time when Stéphan fell down from the gable, broke his back, and died. For that's when the watch stopped.

There are photographs of Pierre and of Jean, separately or with their friends, taken in different parts of the globe, according to how chance and service wash up a sailor on land: Saigon and Amsterdam, Suez and Barcelona. They are as rigid as athletes showing off their muscles, and their eyes are as stiff as those of men condemned to death.

And there are coloured postcards from all sorts of places: the Bay of Naples with its pines and its Vesuvius; Table Mountain; Japanese prostitutes in European bathing-costume, and Tahitian prostitutes in a bit of raffia. Above, in all innocence, hang Jeanne d'Arc and St Anne.

Beside the hearth stands the bench where Tintidil sits when she needs to keep warm. There stands the three-legged iron pot with grey porridge, under which she builds the fire for her own and the cat's and Petit's joint meals. And through the autumn and winter there stand many pieces of wood of varying sizes to dry. They come in all kinds of shapes, and some of them have the remains of paint and letters on them. Tintidil finds them on the beach after there has been a storm, one of the real storms that last for nine days. One morning the ocean becomes calm again, and Tintidil goes out and collects what she can find. Every bit of wood helps in time of war.

The sea provides much. Recently it provided a lump of butter the size of a head, mixed with sand all the way through, but nevertheless useful according to Tintidil. The morning all the corpses of the horses floated in, with the numbers of English regiments branded on their flanks, it provided an oak log as thick as a barrel. Tintidil did not manage to move it from the spot, and others took it.

In the living-room lie the sardine nets. They lie there rotting and rent because they have not been used for more than two years. And out on the grass stands the beached boat, so dried up that one can see right through it: the big, splendid boat in which she and Stéphan once invested everything they owned.

All her life Tintidil has been a strong and able-bodied person. When she gave birth to Jean she kept to her bed for two days. On the third she was again standing knee-deep in water, raking kelp with the other wives. She has never been at all superstitious. But recently she has been unable to sleep.

It is as if she were possessed. No sooner has she raked out the fire and bolted the door for the night than her head starts to whirl as if she had a fever. She crawls into bed, and she crawls out again. The house around her has become so full of strange noises, and she is more aware of them than are Petit and the cat.

She can hear the sea too. Although she has always lived on the shore she had never heard it previously. It must have become more noisy of late, and more wicked. Tintidil is beginning to believe that it has designs on her and wants to take, not just the house, but herself as well.

She has become frightened of everything. Wasn't she so frightened of a light she saw moving the other evening that she sat up all night to see if it appeared again? She takes up her rosary and prays the whole cycle many times. But suddenly she finds herself thinking about the boys again, or about the house, about the nets, about the boat, in the middle of a Pater or an Ave. Even the rosary does not help her any more.

She lights a candle, one of the crooked, peculiar candles she has made out of a lump of tallow that the sea threw up on land once upon a time, and takes up her knitting. But since wool has become so expensive that a pair of socks amounts to seven francs, there is no comfort in that any more. On the contrary.

She goes outside and looks at the weather. Isn't the dawn coming soon? The wall clock moves pitilessly slowly. The first grey light is like deliverance from a nightmare. Once she fell to her knees before the sun, and does not deny it.

Occasionally she is given sleeping-drops in the kitchen before she leaves us at night. She takes them like an obedient child, her mouth open and ready well in advance. Nobody knows whether they are any use. But the next morning she comes quickly up the slope with Petit and assures us in her broken French, 'Tintidil sleep well!'

The trouble is that each time we give Tintidil sleeping-drops we find one of her skinny cockerels on our kitchen table. It lies there plucked and irretrievably dead, with drooping comb and long, corpse-pale claws, and there is nothing to be done about it.

When darkness begins to fall she leaves us. We watch her and Petit getting smaller and smaller as they go downhill. Shortly afterwards we know she is letting herself into the dark little house, alone again with everything collapsing about her, and with the eternal sea.

The sea is never silent. Even when it lies shining like silk it licks at the land with its long tongues. It advances with a hiss and retreats with a deathly sigh so enormous that it fills the vault of heaven. And the pebbles at the low tide-line rattle in it like bones.

Winter has come to Brémoder in the way it does on the coast: without cold, but with gales, with the ocean in uproar, evil and raging, with its tree-stumps and flotsam, lashing rain and a low, dark sky. And with an occasional day that is much too clear, much too calm, bearing fresh storms within it. It blows so that the house gives at the joints, so that the stone walls collapse, so that people cannot stand upright. It rains so that the landscape is altered by it: the roads turn into gullies, the sloping land is washed away and new contours are formed.

There are nights when an unseen hand shakes the house and tries to lift it, when the roof slates clatter against each other and no door can be opened because it feels as if all hell is trying to come in. Mornings when everybody, driven by the same instinct, goes down to the beach. Days when there is a continuous crowd down there, watching the white, frothing lace edge left by the mountainous breakers, before they sink back into the deep.

For it is there in the surf that they first become visible, the black objects that may turn out to be anything: freight, tree-stumps, dead animals or dead people, nobody knows exactly what until they finally lie on the shore, wrested from the undertow.

No sport is more exciting than following the wave when it withdraws, daring to go as close to the black object as possible, to drag it in a short distance, perhaps to rescue it altogether before running for dear life towards land again, pursued by the next moving, roaring mass of water.

Now the ocean is no longer hissing or sighing: it is roaring.

All sounds are drowned in its roar. Humans have to put their lips close to each other's ears and shout loudly if they want to be heard, flocks of gulls and other sea-birds drift out of control, helplessly flapping in to the land, to gather where there is a little shelter: a dishevelled, mincing throng with all their feathers in disarray.

But in the kitchen Marie-Catherine is ironing. Here are steam and warmth from the iron, the sound of newly stiffened tulle between the gusts, young girls coming and going a little shyly, chatting while they wait. It's Saturday afternoon and cosy. Marie-Catherine's big day, when she has a special little expression round her mouth. It comes from her knowing herself to be indispensable.

She is ironing white headdresses, *coiffes*. To get them right is a craft and an art, and gives one status in the village. It must not be neglected because one happens to be in service with some tourists from the city. It is not granted to anyone to put the curve into the little tab behind each ear so that it sits as it should. Girls and housewives come to Marie-Catherine from far away.

And Marie-Catherine tests the iron with a wetted finger so that it hisses, guiding it hither and thither with a practised hand, creating form out of the formless in the time it takes to count to three. She has taken off her own *coiffe*, as she usually does when she works, and stands there in the tiny black skull-cap that holds her tightly combed hair far back on the crown of her head. With the long line of her neck rising from the low, close-fitting waist of her dress, her shoulders enclosing it, her brown complexion and high, arching forehead, Marie-Catherine might have belonged in an early Florentine painting, if it were not for her nose, which is in decided opposition to all the rest. And for the small, rough, hardened working hands. Nobody can match her in holding out courageously and cheerfully when it is required.

A big, buxom girl is sitting, smiling and flushed, in the chair beside the kitchen door: Joséphine, newly married. Leave can be used in many ways. When Tintimarianna's son came home last time they took advantage of it to slaughter the pig. But Joséphine's sweetheart used his six days to get married and install Joséphine in the one room of his family's house. Now she is going round with a shining new ring on her finger, herself shining and new through and through, getting two francs twenty-five a day in support as a soldier's wife. Absolutely free, as Marie-Catherine says.

The wedding was a quiet one, as the situation demanded, without any singing or dancing, only the closest relatives. Perhaps that is why Joséphine starts singing when she has sat for a while: first, a low humming; then, when we encourage her, at the top of her lungs. There's a gale blowing; we are alone. And Joséphine needs to sing; she hasn't been allowed to sing yet. In spite of everything she believes in happiness; one can see and hear it. Now she is making up for lost time. We are given the long story about St Anne and the even longer one about the Wandering Jew. But finally we are given love songs, the ones that have been sung for centuries at weddings and would have been sung at Joséphine's wedding, had it not been for the war.

Ho karout a rann koulskoude
Enn hoc'h e sonnjan noz ha de
Ho alan, dre doull ann alc'houe
A zeu d'am dihun em gwele.*

Here Joséphine pauses, for someone is coming. For a while afterwards we can hear only the storm. And then Marie-Catherine starts to talk about the fallen. If she had been thinking about Joséphine, she would certainly not have done so, but at this moment Marie-Catherine is thinking about herself.

From the neighbouring farm, Fantenigou, a total of seven men have gone to the war. One has returned. His face is destroyed. There is no face there any more, only a scarred wound. He seldom goes out, but finds things to do indoors. He

* And yet I love thee still, / night and day I think of no other; / thy breath reacheth me through the keyhole / and waketh me when I sleep.

is twenty-five years old.

The others will not return. They 'stayed out there'.

Marie-Catherine mentions a few more examples. Then she says, 'People used to say that there were ten girls for every boy from Pointe du Raz to Penmarch. How many are there now?'

She bends deeper over her work and presses her lips tightly together.

Towards evening the gale drops, and we go out.

The ocean is grey as lead under a yellow-grey sky, the sandbanks pallid in the twilight, the drizzle dank. Clogs are clattering along the wet lanes, all going in the same direction, to the churchyard at Plouhinec. Tomorrow it is All Souls' Day, the day when no grave should look neglected.

In the sickly, fading light the women of the parish busy themselves among the graves, each as best she can. Some have brought wreaths of glass beads, but not many. Most of them are carrying something in a bundle, which they put down carefully and untie. And they strew the grave with white sand from the beach, decorate it with a pattern of snail shells and pretty stones on top of the sand, then plant the last rose or geranium from the autumn flowering in their windows in the centre.

Here lie old seafarers, work-worn mothers, an occasional young person who died of disease: people who died peacefully in their beds.

But alongside, on a grassy slope below the churchyard wall, decorations are brought for those who do not lie here, those who 'stayed' at sea or 'over there'.

Quietly and busily the women's hands pat together small sand heaps and arrange their flowers and snail shells. They look like small gardens, children's allotments.

And with their faces hidden behind the blinkers of their mourning bonnets, mothers, wives, sweethearts and sisters kneel side by side in the driving rain, make the sign of the cross and pray silently, each beside her tiny little bed.

There's a War On

Night. Pitch darkness. Not a ray of light betrays the fact that people live here, masses of people, millions of them; that they are packed together like bees in a honeycomb, beside each other and on top of each other in cell beside cell, cell above cell; that this is a metropolis.

At long intervals greyness falls on a section of pavement. A street lamp is burning there, turned low, wearing a large black hat. The glow it casts is apportioned so miserly, so thinned down and rubbed out, that it is not much more than a smudge in the darkness, a discolouration.

But the light comes, cleaving the night like a blade, hacking into it in all directions. It is met by other blades. As if combining to impale some object, they pursue each other all over the sky. And a wailing breaks out, brutal, idiotic, an insult against all reason, all calm, all quiet effort. In the murk at the bottom of the chasms of the streets it bellows out on two notes, stressing the second: *doo, doo-oo, doo, doo-oo, doo, doo-oo. . . .*

Black shadows dart from lamp to lamp. Behind them the darkness folds up completely and is universal. The blades of light remain in its boundlessness, meet, accompany one another, part, meet again and suddenly stand still at a tiny point, nothing but a dot, while the wailing continues to bellow at the bottom of the chasm.

When it is again possible to distinguish sounds, the drone of a motor can be heard from out in space.

No outward sign betrays it, but now the houses have come to life, an inner, whispering, stealthy life. People are coming out of the doors at all levels. Ghostly figures, people dressed in only the most necessary clothing – a nightdress, a warm coat – with flashlights directed at one another as if at burglars, are shuffling down the stairs. But some merely open the door a crack and look out at the others. And some do not open up at all.

Old people are helped down, step by step, sleeping children are carried: big, sleeping children, who have become used to being dragged awake, and have made up their minds to sleep in spite of everything.

The wailing has stopped. A stillness as if before a storm has succeeded it. The slightest sound can be heard in it, and the people are as sensitive to them as animals or wild things. They listen, as they listened in caves and catacombs, when night and danger allied themselves together and encircled them. They exchange a few words now and then, attacking the stillness, but under their breath as if to avoid being outwitted by whatever it is out there. They light candles, tiny, flickering flames, grouped in cellars as in chapels, blink sleepily at them and yawn, exchange a few words again, trying to see each other through the gloom: 'Are you there?'

'Yes, are *you* there?'

'A nice how-d'ye-do!'

'There's a war on.'

But some of them choose to retreat into the darkness.

'What's that?'

'Nothing. A door banging. There it goes again.'

Madame Leroux and old Monsieur Dubois. Madame Leroux is always the first to hear things, and Monsieur Dubois the one to counteract it. He is sitting there with a certain responsibility for the whole cellar and for the atmosphere in it. Nervousness must not be allowed to spread.

Mlle Leroux is not present; Mlle Leroux is lying in her bed.

She stands from morning till night in one of the big department stores and refuses to budge now. But Madame Leroux has other children, she has a son at the war, and can find no peace either upstairs or down.

'Sit down, madame,' counsels Monsieur Dubois, offering her a camp-stool. 'One must be a fatalist. It's the only way.'

'Are you a fatalist?' asks Madame Leroux drily, refusing to sit down. Monsieur Dubois is a childless old man and ought to abstain from such remarks.

There is a distant explosion.

'There they are!'

'No, that was a gun. It was one of ours.'

Another explosion.

'This time . . .'

'Yes, this time . . .'

'There are several of them, more than one.'

An explosion close by, making the air vibrate.

'My daughter!' cries Madame Leroux. But Madame Bourg puts her knitting down in her lap and asks after Bernard. He ought to be here by now.

Madame Bourg always knits: one thick, man's sock after the other, in the cellar as well. The clicking of her needles is domestic, reassuring, a pleasant little sound with something enduring about it. After each explosion it surfaces exactly as before. Like the practised family knitter she is, Madame Bourg casts off and decreases almost without looking at what she is doing. With the yarn hooked over her finger and a knitting-needle stuck in her mouth, she lifts her work up to the light for a moment, leans forward slightly, mutters, and it is done. She sits there again, with an absorbed, patient expression. Now and again it is as if she gathers her wits: she looks about her, pursing her lips maternally at the children who, lying on their mothers' laps, are sleeping again after the explosions; she searches in the darkness for those who are sitting there with no children on their laps, because they are somewhere quite different; she asks after Bernard.

'We can hear him coming' is the reply from the staircase.

Bernard always comes last. But then he does live right at the top of the house, on the sixth floor. He has a long way to come, and he arrives in procession, bringing a large proportion of his belongings with him.

He is really called, quite simply, Bernhardt. But in the country in which he finds himself his name becomes Bernard. The country is at war; the war is being fought in the country, not so very far from the city where Bernard resides. He is involved just as much as the others, moving perpetually down six floors and up six floors, and must be presumed to hear both sirens and bombs. Nevertheless he is outside, apart from it all, understanding nothing, but is, so far as is known, neither blind, nor deaf, nor dumb.

He is three weeks old.

When his basket appears on the cellar stairs, illuminated from below, several pairs of arms stretch out to receive him. 'Let me!' 'No, let me, I can do it more easily.' 'Thank God he's here!'

An exhausted young man, without a tie and with his collar turned up – besides old Monsieur Dubois he is the only man in the whole cellar, and definitely the only *young* man – slings him down. Then an exhausted, distracted mother arrives. She nods her thanks in silence to these helpful people, and simply sits down and stares at Bernard. 'He ought not to be in the air of the cellar so much,' she occasionally mutters dazedly to herself. Or, 'He ought to have sun.'

Two irresponsible young artists from Scandinavia, who hadn't the good sense to get back home in time, and were even more lacking in sense when they went and acquired Bernard in the middle of all this. But now it has happened, and a child is a child. The unfortunate little family have become the centre of attention in the cellar, even though they ought to have stayed where they came from with their painting and child rearing in times like these, when able-bodied young men are lying out in the trenches among rats and lice, in blood and mud, shooting and being shot, and when every drop of milk and every pat of butter, every piece of coal, every gramme of flour and sugar are in short supply.

But never mind about that. It's not Bernard's fault. And in this situation, only a monster would say anything.

When he appeared in the cellar for the first time he was like all infants, and nine days old. Now he is almost smaller than when he arrived, his cry more miserable and more angry, his sleep restless. When he opens his eyes they are more expressive than they should be, with an experienced and reproachful look that has an unnatural effect in a baby's face. His tiny fingers are blue as if Bernard is always freezing, even though he is well wrapped up, with hot-water bottles around him. To say it plainly, Bernard is starving.

As if to emphasize his untimely arrival in this world, the powers that be have cut off the sources of his nourishment. Nothing helps, not even the bean flour that bedouin women use in the desert, and which Madame Bourg has got hold of. His mother sits there, lacking sleep, looking as if she were guilty of dereliction of duty. And whatever Bernard gets instead is not much use, however carefully they weigh it and measure it out. He drinks ravenously, and – a belch – he is empty again. He looks up with reproachful eyes, sucks in empty air, screams. He has not given up, but fights for his existence as best he can.

Mlle Blanchard brings up the rear of the procession, laden like a pack-horse. She lives on the same floor as Bernard and helps to carry things. Nobody has more than two hands. Bernard's father carries the baby basket with his. His mother has to hold on to the banisters with the one, and in the other she has the stand with the bottles, prepared ready. Who would carry the baby clothes and the primus and the powder and the ointment and the rest of it if not Mlle Blanchard? A visit to the cellar can last for minutes or hours. If the house is hit, it may be days before they can get out of the ruins; there have been plenty of examples of that. In such a situation one must be able to hold out as long as possible.

Like certain waiters Mlle Blanchard has become adept at carrying the most incredible number of objects, and at putting them down without mishap. Only then does she think of her own concerns and disappears into a dark corner, where she is noticed subsequently only because of a slight rattling, the sound of her rosary as she sits telling the beads.

She is not the kind who is good at bending over Bernard and making expert remarks. Nor does she pretend she can. But she knows how to carry things, and what she knows about, she does.

In fact Mlle Blanchard does more for Bernard than most of the others in the cellar. But as happens frequently, others reap the praise. Madame Bourg reaps the most, even though it is far from her intention to put anyone in the shade. She can give advice, she calls his mother *mon enfant* and Bernard *notre p'tit vieux*, lifting him out of his basket in the way he ought to be lifted, so that his head doesn't loll and his back is properly supported, doing it fearlessly and firmly, quite differently from his mother, who is anxious and fumbling.

Madame Bourg has sons herself. Like all mothers she loves looking back, cherishing the memory of a helplessness so great that it laid total claim on her, and of progress that did not yet threaten to lead away from her. She looks at Bernard and says, 'Pierre at that age . . .', 'Louis at that age. . . .' Perhaps she forgets for a moment that Pierre and Louis are grown boys and gone to the war. Then she must remember it again, for she sighs.

But Mlle Blanchard is in the post office and for years has been a good daughter and supported and finally buried her widowed mother. Mlle Blanchard can wield pens and die-stamps, that's her province; she can be patient with old people and read boring things aloud to them. The longer the war lasts, the fewer are her chances of ever experiencing anything else. Her generation is condemned to spinsterhood and barrenness; it can already be demonstrated statistically. In fact they might just as well withdraw into the shadows at once, so that it is done voluntarily, so to speak, and with dignity. If it were not for Bernard, Mlle Blanchard, too, would perhaps be in her bed, like Mlle Leroux, like many along with her. In resignation, in disgust.

She had wished to go out and nurse the wounded, had wished to become part of a greater unity and feel that she was doing so. But a woman in the post office is needed in the postal service now more than ever. Everyone said so, and she heard it wherever she turned. She remained at the window in the dark, old-fashioned post office in the side-street. Another quiet deed of heroism, like everything else that Mlle Blanchard undertakes in this world.

The employment of a person who might be able to save Bernard is out of the question for the unfortunates in the attic. It does not occur to anyone to suggest such a thing. Besides, the country women are no longer earning their living by meeting the requirements of the city; they can't, even if they were promised the moon. They are needed behind plough and harrow, spade and fork, everywhere where the men left off. They can't even be found, but have gone home, leaving everyone in the lurch.

All those who can, have left, and rightly. At least it means fewer mouths to feed. In the country there is peace and quiet, fresh air and sunshine, all sorts of possibilities. Bernard ought to leave too. The doctor has said so, everyone says so, Bernard's parents admit it. But to take action, to find documents, travel permits, seats on one of the overcrowded trains – all the things that take time and must be begun as soon as possible, these they do not do. Nobody drops hints about it any more.

Madame Bourg has made inquiries privately at the nearest children's hospital. It was overcrowded. And then there was the matter of the country women. Nobody can force them to stay. The few who were left were far from sufficient. But if Madame Bourg tried another hospital, in another part of the city, then perhaps. . . .

Madame Bourg went home. It is impossible to carry Bernard to distant parts of the city. Even if there are trams, they are subject to the fortunes of war. A hole in the street, a torn-up rail, and they are brought to a standstill.

It has become ridiculous to hide in the cellar. Fewer and fewer people bother. One would have to live there. No sooner are you back in bed than the alarm goes again. It goes in the daytime. Destruction swoops from a clear sky, a sky without a speck in it and in full sunshine, makes craters in the asphalt, explodes and is gone. It's beyond human understanding. People stare upwards, fail to reach any conclusion, then return to their affairs. If one cannot do anything else, one can at least do that, contribute to law and order. The eleven-year-old girl on the third floor is called back from the window and made to play her C major scale over again. That's her contribution.

Then somebody finds a piece of a missile. The mystery is a gun. A phenomenon of a gun, of which the world has never seen the like before in its ability to shoot far.

It is obvious to the most inexperienced that Bernard's stay in this inhospitable life seriously threatens to be short. He still uses his strength, such as it is, to protest; when he is asleep he drinks in his dreams, so he can be heard all over the cellar. But he plucks at the sheet with tiny, restless fingers, a gesture that has become a habit, whether it is a helpless attempt to get what nobody can provide him with, or the fumbling of the dying for something to cling to.

His mother sits staring at him, as if she is trying to hold him fast in her gaze. His father? He trudges round half the city looking for milk, stands in queues for hours, and in between comes home again empty-handed. An infant's ration does not go very far on the days when supplies are lacking. He glances at Bernard, looks away again and down at the floor. If he is thinking that maybe it would be better if it were all over, this is perhaps no more than human.

'What if we were to fetch Ernestine?'

It is a night when the stillness that follows the alarm signal seems never-ending. It hovers intolerably between the cellar walls, interrupted only by Bernard's perpetual sucking in his dream and his sudden small cries of misery. Nobody talks, even Mlle Blanchard's rosary is not rattling. Nothing is happening outside. No explosions, no all-clear. The little group of people who still – whether from old habit or for Bernard's sake – go down to the cellar, seem forgotten down there.

But suddenly thin little Madame Mialon, from the first floor above the courtyard, who works as a domestic help and is the most reserved, the least domineering of them all, appears in the middle of the room, with a proposal. And what a proposal! As simple as fitting a sock to the foot and daring as an emergency manoeuvre. 'What if we were to fetch Ernestine? Her youngest is fourteen months, and he's like *this*.' Madame Mialon's gesture implies something decidedly round. She is speaking louder than before, with increasing assurance.

'Ernestine?' Madame Bourg drops her knitting.

'The wife of the caretaker in No. 30, madame. Four children. As healthy as you and me. If I hadn't been afraid of seeming to interfere, I'd have suggested it long ago.'

'He ought, at any rate, to have hydrotherapy first,' says Madame Bourg, feeling her way.

'Doctors' invention, madame. We don't need to make such a fuss. He's hungry. He needs food, not water.'

Silence.

Madame Bourg takes off her spectacles and polishes the lens. This is no easy matter. No, God knows. Much is concealed in it, the one problem within the other. She turns towards Bernard's basket. 'You will have to decide, mes enfants,' she says, strangely tired.

Decide? Two distracted, exhausted faces look up at each other. Then old Monsieur Dubois speaks with the voice of authority. 'If she will come, this Madame Ernestine, it seems to me that there is no choice to be made. It's a matter of alternatives, isn't it?'

'That's my opinion precisely,' says Madame Mialon.

Madame Bourg looks into the half-dark again, where the mother is sitting. And the mother nods, her eyes shining with tears.

'Go and ask her!' says Madame Bourg. 'One can always ask.'

Madame Mialon disappears up the stairs and out into the darkness, quick on her feet as a rat, used to making the least possible noise when she comes and goes. And the stillness is there again, worse than ever, burdened with doubt and uncertainty. When finally there can be heard a rustle of skirts, children's tripping feet, a whining and scolding at the entrance to the cellar, it feels like a deliverance. It really is Ernestine. Fate wills that it is she.

'My husband's at the war, and I have four children,' she announces by way of introduction. 'I'm not leaving them, here they are. If anything should happen, it's best we all go. All at once. In addition I'm a caretaker's wife. I'm risking my job by leaving the house in the middle of the night.'

She stands in the glow of the candle that Madame Bourg is holding up, an ordinary looking person, of average height, average width, not very good tempered and with a sturdy, sleeping child in her arms. Three more are clinging to her skirts, rubbing their eyes sleepily with their fists, and whining.

'There's a war on,' says Madame Bourg, with a sudden smile; an experienced smile of complicity, as one who has immediately sized up Ernestine and knows her.

'There's a war on. We must help one another. Here I am. Where is this lady and her child?'

Madame Bourg shines the light on Bernard, on the whole pathetic little group. And Ernestine's severe caretaker's expression breaks up into a motherly pursing of the lips. 'Heavens above, look at him!'

Then she hands over the sturdy child to other arms, lifts Bernard out of the basket and sits down comfortably with him. She scolds him and slaps his bottom to get him going. And then an explosion shakes the walls.

In the stillness that follows, Ernestine's children's howling is the first sound. 'Be quiet, Pierre! Shut up, Simone! Don't roar like that, Jean! We're all of us here, can't you see?'

Then there follows a sound, a tiny sound of life itself, present in spite of the clamour of death: the regular gurgling of a baby sucking and finding nourishment.

The cellar holds its breath and listens, not to what is happening outside, but inside. Face after face moves into the meagre glow of the candle, stays there a moment, staring with open mouth, then gives way to another. Something is happening that is right and proper, something is beginning to grow as women think it should grow; nothing is being destroyed, something is being protected. Mlle Blanchard says over and over, 'He's drinking, he's drinking!' Old Monsieur Dubois keeps to the fringe so that the women may watch; he is rubbing his hands with pleasure. Once or twice the tiny sound is drowned by an explosion, but it surfaces again.

Someone has found an oil-lamp. It is standing on a crate shining richly and steadily on Bernard and Ernestine who are combined in a figure of total serenity. Ernestine's surly, everyday expression is composed and still and beautiful. She, like many another, might be a madonna.

Among the other faces, the mother's. It is as if she, too, is drinking. New life is streaming beneath her skin into her features, into her eyes. And the father's, a mask of harsh defiance, gradually dissolving.

Suddenly Bernard is asleep. He has not taken so very much, but he has decided to sleep on it, to put it to use. Ernestine gets cautiously to her feet and puts him in the basket. It is a decisive moment.

Bernard is asleep. The tiny fingers are quite still, splayed out motionless above the sheet. The magical peace that streams out from a sleeping child is already in the atmosphere, shared to a greater or lesser degree by them all.

'Well, I declare – I think I'm fond of him already,' says Ernestine.

Together with Bernard, his mother has fallen asleep. With her head on her husband's shoulder she sleeps as profoundly and quietly as her child. She is not awakened by the next explosion, nor by the signal announcing the all-clear.

Madame

She has gone and everyone is relieved, human nature being what it is.

This place is really for the elderly, a so-called quiet place. Here respectable rubbers of bridge are played, but even more often they play patience, knit lovely soft scarves and show photographs of grandchildren. The radio is not switched on at any time of day, only when there is something really interesting on the programme. And bedtime is early.

Any young people who find their way here are of the undemanding, non-dancing type, often the kind who are prepared to sacrifice themselves for others by nursing the sick or caring for souls. A few, come to recover from some illness, to study for an exam they have failed, or who, like Mr Ahrén, are from Sweden and have a university degree, are the exceptions. But never to such an extent as Madame.

Not that she was noisy or had a challenging personality. On the contrary, Madame was quiet. To start with there was really nothing she could be criticized for, even though some people said all sorts of things. But then she did invite it.

This motoring, for instance. Madame was always phoning for a car. To go for a drive? Far from it. To go to the store, the chemist, the newsagent, and home again. It took about five minutes, perhaps eight or ten if she had to stand and wait anywhere. Making allowance for all eventualities Madame could have gone the rounds on foot in fifteen or twenty minutes. And it would have done her more good than sitting in her room all day, and then wandering about till eleven or twelve o'clock at night, waking everyone in the vicinity with creaking stairs, running water, and objects dropped on the floor.

She sat in the car as if preparing to be out for hours, leaning well back, one leg crossed over the other, her hands in large cuffed gloves folded in her lap and her gaze focused far away. She descended the stairs *dressed up*, having changed, and put on a hat and different shoes. She drew on her gloves as she came. She slammed the car door behind her and made a distrait gesture to let Tønnessen know that he could drive off.

All this out in the country. It couldn't help but give rise to criticism. Everyone had her own theory concerning the phenomenon. Madame was an upstart, showing off, trying to impress. Madame was getting divorced and was suffering from divorce psychosis. Madame was an adventuress with an adventuress's habits. Indeed, it was to be hoped that Madame was not out-and-out *demi-mondaine*.

But Tønnessen winked cunningly at the bystanders when he swung the car round to the steps with Madame and her many small packages, newspapers and magazines. In his eyes she was simply an eccentric.

At times she scarcely touched her food. On the other hand she would turn up repeatedly at the wrong time of the day asking for something to eat. As if this were a hotel and all you had to do was to give orders. At first a tray or two were brought to her room, and she sat up there eating an omelette, for instance, when everyone else had had meat balls or lamb and cabbage stew for dinner. It gave rise to dissatisfaction, and could not continue indefinitely.

When Madame was first introduced, the proprietress got lost in a thicket of consonants and came no further. Madame shrugged her shoulders icily, a gesture she often used, and said the name herself. Nobody caught it correctly, even though she repeated it when asked. The register was no help, since Madame's handwriting was pure scribble. Lund, the old headmaster, finally decided that the name must be Polish, and that Madame was written in front of it, not Mrs. So she became Madame, when addressed or talked about.

Otherwise she spoke Norwegian like one of us, possibly searching occasionally for certain words. When she talked at all, that is, for she was not easy to converse with. It was impossible to keep a conversation going with Madame, everyone agreed about that. She replied absent-mindedly and at cross purposes, indeed so foolishly at times that one was forced to ask oneself what kind of a person she was. She evidenced no interests of any kind. She seemed to be a complete outsider. And God knows what this supposed Polish marriage involved. She never mentioned husband or home. If anyone tried, cautiously and tactfully, to find out, she gave the impression that she had not understood.

Was she handsome? Oh, no. A thin, anguished face. On the other hand it could not be denied that she was well dressed, worryingly, irritatingly well dressed, as is the lot of only the fortunate few: simply, expensively and correctly.

Those ladies who had long ago acquired incurably large stomachs, buttocks and upper arms from too much sitting, involuntarily straightened their backs and drew in what muscles they could, fore and aft, when Madame's figure, slender as an eel in exclusive clothes and discreet make-up, came into sight. Her hair was fashioned as if she were a lady of society in *Vogue* or *The Tatler*. You could see your reflection in her nails.

And one day Madame fainted.

She suddenly rose from the table and had come as far as the door when it happened. With her slim hand she gripped the door frame for support, then sank slowly to the floor and lay there, her head on the threshold and her feet in the hall.

There was a tremendous fuss and palaver.

Madame lay there so elegantly, not all of a heap, as can so easily happen in such cases, but with one knee up, one arm bent backwards in an arc about her head, her hair like a halo beneath it, and a long, elegant silk leg visible right up to her thigh. If it had not been obvious before how slender and exquisite and exclusive, how gentle and light her body really was, it certainly was obvious then. She lay there like an injured film star.

It was an unexpected piece of good fortune that Mr Ahrén had arrived. Normally the male element consists, for long stretches of the year, of Lund, the old headmaster, who comes regularly for several months at a time. He can't manage to do very much, poor thing. Very kindly and without wasting time Mr Ahrén did what obviously had to be done. He gathered up Madame and carried her to a sofa. After a moment's hesitation, a little clumsily and unused to such a situation, he also arranged her legs properly and put a cushion under her head. Then he assumed a waiting attitude.

The proprietress arrived with brandy. She had heard that this was the best thing for faints. When she failed to get it down Madame's throat, she splashed it over her on the outside, on her temples and elsewhere.

Relief that the accident had occurred before Madame had reached the staircase was great and generally shared. It could have been a matter of life and limb. Some also remarked that it was a mercy her colour was so normal. Madame was always pale, and she was no paler now than usual. Nor was she flushed, as happens to some. She was unaltered, and neither cold nor hot, but just right.

It was decided that peace and quiet were the only remedy. And that Madame must start going to bed like other people and eating like other people. This exaggerated slimming – they died of it over there in Hollywood, after all. And not surprising either, if it made you so weak.

Mr Ahrén gathered up Madame once more and carried her in procession to her bed. There she opened her eyes and looked about her with astonishment. She said nothing.

Was she feeling a little better?

'Yes, thank you.'

Was she in the habit of fainting?

'No, never.'

Perhaps there was something the matter that ought to be attended to?

Madame stared briefly at the ceiling. 'My appendix,' she murmured eventually.

Aha, she was weak after the operation! Why hadn't she mentioned it, then? A couple of the ladies, who had had their appendix removed, suddenly recognized the situation well. Good heavens, how little we understand one another! Here she had been sitting day after day unable to get any food inside her. People all around her, the murmur of voices, heat, movement. She ought to eat in her room for a while, poor soul, perhaps go on a diet. Since everyone knew the reason, there couldn't be anything the matter.

There was nothing the matter. A sudden atmosphere of goodwill sprang up around Madame. The appendix explained a great deal, even the car trips. It was true that Madame went out walking for hours in the evening, but that was quite different. Then it was neither dusty nor hot.

'Thank you so much,' said Madame to the suggestion that she should take her meals in her room.

For a while they scarcely saw anything of her. They saw the trays being carried up from the kitchen and disappearing along the corridor. It gave rise to general anxiety when they came back almost untouched.

She still ordered the car now and again. They saw her entering and leaving it. Otherwise they ran into Madame only in the evening twilight. She came and went like a ghost, thin and noiseless in her flat-heeled shoes and her light grey ulster, which she wrapped around her as if freezing. Individuals with intitiative would call to her to ask how she was. 'Thank you, much better,' answered Madame.

Those with even more initiative went up and knocked on her door, to visit her in her room, for the poor thing was really very much alone. But no conversation resulted from that either. So they gave up.

One afternoon they found her lying in a faint in the corridor outside Mr Ahrén's door. Another fortunate accident. He heard her fall, raised the alarm and carried her in procession to her bed. Then he left, after muttering something about 'a strange case'. It almost seemed as if he had had enough of gathering up Madame and carrying her to where she belonged.

He who was usually so polite! But he was staying here in order to write his thesis and naturally could not make himself readily available.

The reason why Mr Ahrén repeatedly comes back to this quiet, out-of-the-way place is that his mother came from the area. And if you are to forsake the world awhile for the sake of your studies, you may as well do so thoroughly.

He is an exceptionally handsome, very tall young man, extremely correct, with such an elegant bow. It is unthinkable that a hasty word should ever pass his lips. The elderly ladies fall for him because of his calm personality, the younger ones because he is so tall, and in addition Swedish and reserved. He is always given the same room, and is altogether the pride of the guest-house, accompanied as he is by the aura of important and unusual circumstance. Now he was behaving less perfectly than usual.

One of the ladies turned to him and suggested, thinking of Madame's unaltered complexion, 'Do you think this *is* a fainting fit? Don't you think it might be a touch of epilepsy?'

'Very likely,' replied Mr Ahrén so coldly and curtly that she was quite astonished. And he was gone.

Now there was a lot of talk about the doctor. He ought to be summoned immediately. Madame was beginning to fall about all over the place, now here, now there. Think of the stairs! And there was no hospital in the vicinity. Madame ought to go into a convalescent home, weak as she was.

Meanwhile Madame had revived and was staring, round-eyed, at the gathering. 'I must have fallen again,' she remarked quietly.

Yes, she had fallen again, and frightened the life out of them all. But now they were going to phone the nice, kind doctor in the village.

'No!' Madame gestured away from herself with her beautiful slender hand. She had been careless just now, had wanted to go out, although she had felt tired. It would not happen again. But no doctor – she was so tired of doctors . . .

'Perhaps Madame ought to stay in bed for a few days,' said someone. 'Until she gets her strength back.'

'Perhaps I ought,' said Madame, looking almost perplexed.

The idea was clearly strange to her. It gave rise to general and unconditional agreement. Of course Madame ought to stay in bed! Fancy nobody thinking of that before!

So Madame was shut in.

A week passed. Madame was invisible, almost forgotten.

One evening at around midnight one of the elderly ladies sat up in bed, listened for a while, put on her slippers and her dressing-gown and left her room. She knocked quietly on doors, whispered through them, managed to wake another guest and the proprietress. Three elderly women, out of humour and in their negligées, with small wispy pigtails down their backs, shuffled in single file along the corridors and staircases. Somebody or something had collapsed with a thud on to the floor above. Afterwards there was no sound, which was even more frightening.

But if it was Madame again, things really were going too far. Wasn't she going to leave them in peace at night either?

It was Madame. She was lying on the floor of her room. She had overturned a chair in her fall. The door was ajar.

From the dark corridor the interior looked like a painting. In the background the window, open on to the blue night, farther forward the table with a bowl of late summer flowers attractively lit by the glow of the shaded lamp, and pretty little items of luxury scattered about. In the shadow the bed, elegant pieces of clothing draped over the back of a chair, the glitter of silver and crystal on the glass shelf above the wash-basin. And in the foreground Madame, more like an injured film star than ever. Luscious bottle-green pyjamas, small green slippers on naked feet, one knee bent, one arm arched backwards around her head, and so on. The three shuffling figures came upon it so suddenly that they were startled.

They gathered her up. It was not easy. Not as when Mr Ahrén lifted her in his strong arms. In the meanwhile their brains were working fast. A remark that Ahrén, too, could not have failed to hear something, since there was only an empty room between him and Madame, probed like a feeler that is extended quickly and suddenly drawn in again. Nobody replied.

They stood round the bed, breathing heavily and looking at Madame. One of her slippers had fallen off, and a slender, fine-boned foot, well cared for and supple, sensitive and as full of expression as a hand, with skin like silk and nails like polished agate, lay on the rug. It told one more about Madame than her face did. It called openly for tenderness, for caresses and kisses. But only the three with the pigtails saw it, and it startled them for the second time, as if they had seen something revolting. One of them hastened to cover it.

When Madame opened her eyes a change of residence was suggested, without mincing matters. It would be best for her, best for them all. She surely understood that people had the right to peace and quiet at night, especially in this place where people paid dearly in order to rest. Besides, nobody could continue to accept the responsibility if a doctor were not sent for. He must come the very next day.

The doctor came, a pleasant country doctor, used to dealing with a variety of ailments, from amputations and deliveries to toothache and stitch and nerves.

He was escorted upstairs and acquainted with the case on the way. When he came down again he went into the office, talked to the proprietress and made a telephone call. Then he made for his car at once, but was surrounded and detained on the steps.

He shrugged his shoulders vaguely and his statements were cautious. It looked as if all he was going to say was 'We-ell. . . .' Finally he came out with it. What was to be done with the lady? When people are neither ill nor well and belong neither here nor there, it's not easy to know what to do about them. It was clear that she had moved about a good deal, at home and abroad, and she refused to return anywhere, whatever her reasons might be. There was a private rest-home in the next village, a quiet, satisfactory place, ladies only, the superintendent a trained nurse – Madame had agreed that he should book a room for her there. She was not enthusiastic about it, but presumably she wasn't enthusiastic about anything. One would have to hope for the best.

'But what about her appendix, Doctor?' said someone.

'Appendix? Nothing the matter with Madame's appendix.'

'But she's had it removed.'

'Well, so have a good many people, but they're in good health in spite of that.'

'But the operation, Doctor? Surely that's why she's so poorly?'

'The operation? To judge by the scar, that must have been done several years ago, ten or twelve perhaps. No reason to connect that with Madame's present condition. Has anyone done so?'

'Yes, Madame did.'

The doctor shrugged his shoulders again. He seemed to think it was all a lot of nonsense. He got into his car and drove away. He was busy, he said.

And finally the word 'hysteria' was dropped, like a ripe fruit from the bough. Wasn't that what some of them had been thinking? One is so afraid of implying such things.

And how they had indulged her! That type should not be indulged. On the contrary, discipline is best for them, or at any rate firmness.

Madame was ordered to stay in bed until the moment of her departure. She was not to move out of it unless it was absolutely necessary. Because she would risk falling several times more.

Only one night left. Madame was leaving the next morning. They were nearly rid of her. At half-past midnight she fell to the floor.

The lady in the room beneath assured everybody afterwards that she had been expecting it, so it had really not woken her up. But she had struggled hard with herself before getting out of bed. The best for Madame would have been to be left lying there, until there was nothing else for it but to get up again. On the other hand, it takes moral courage to decide on such a course. The nights were chilly already, and then perhaps the window was open and Madame had thin pyjamas. If the outcome were pneumonia it would be no joke.

One of the servants was woken this time, as well as the proprietress. The expedition set off, on tiptoe in slippers and far from kindly in disposition. They came upon Madame a little way along the corridor, midway between Mr Ahrén's door and her own, which was standing wide open against the same familiar backdrop: the window open to the blue night, flowers under the lamp, elegant underwear elegantly draped, and so on. Madame herself was lying as usual, but with both arms thrown backwards this time, and without slippers. Her extraordinarily well-manicured feet, the most beautiful feature of Madame, looked exceedingly out of place on the rough matting. It was painful to see.

The servant, poor soul, was a bit out of things. She asked quite inocently whether it would not be best to knock on Mr Ahrén's door and get him to give them a hand?

'No indeed' came the answer curtly and unsympathetically. 'Mr Ahrén would certainly not be so naïve as to come and help now. He knew what he was doing. If there was anything people could see through, it was that kind of behaviour. Everyone ought really to do the same as he – let Madame lie until she got up again. But there you are, one can't help being sympathetic and kind. Gracious, what a weight! Whew! And at this time of night!'

They huffed and puffed, they scolded and fussed, pulled and tugged and finally tipped their burden on to the bed. Slim, slight Madame became as heavy as a sack of potatoes in their hands.

'Difficult age,' they said. 'About thirty,' they said. 'And when there's a lack of will-power . . . ,' they said. In fact, their patience was exhausted. Loneliness is a suggestive word that perhaps might have occurred to them, and caused them to fall silent. Everyone, as a result of his own experience, can interpret it as he likes, can nod significantly at the idea, and hold various opinions about it. But they had been dragged from their comfortable beds for the second time, and spoke indiscreetly as one does at dead of night.

Madame didn't so much as flutter her eyelids. She didn't even give a start as if jolted awake, not even when she opened her eyes to the sight of three ageing women staring at her, inevitable as in a dream play. She turned away from them and gazed at the ceiling.

And she was asked in a roundabout way, could she explain

what she was doing in the corridor? In the middle of the night? The WC was not in that direction, but quite the other way.

Madame went on gazing at the ceiling.

They spread the blankets over her a little too firmly and quickly, picked up two items of the elegant clothing that had fallen to the floor, and looked about them disapprovingly. Then they left.

The old servant was the last to go. She understand nothing, but she must have thought that Madame was looking small and peaky and thin. In uncertain and confused sympathy she laid her hand for a moment on Madame's forehead, and gave her cheek a couple of pats as if to a child. Then Madame seized her hand with both of her own, stopped gazing at the ceiling, and looked gratefully into the kind, simple eyes.

In the morning Tønnessen brought the car and drove Madame away for the last time. They disappeared round the bend in the road that led down to the station.

Avalanche

They sit silent under the lamp, he reading, she sewing. The stillness about them is heavy with unspoken words, with everything they have been closing their lips over tightly in the course of the day. It is like a substance that thickens and piles up until it seems insurmountable.

He puts down the paper, takes a turn about the room. My God, as long as he doesn't start humming, she thinks. I can't stand it this evening. I'll scream out loud.

He for his part is thinking that when she sits like that with a furrow between her eyes and her mouth in a straight line, sewing silently, she is indeed no flower along life's way, and certainly no light to lighten one's path. She's an affliction. The vague longing, always lying in wait, for something new, something young, stirs in him. He turns away from her, unable to look at her.

But he has to find something to do. 'That little cactus is rather amusing,' he remarks firmly, assaulting the confounded silence. He sits down, crosses one leg over the other and swings it hopefully.

But one can never be cautious enough when launching such assaults.

'What was the idea, bringing me that? I can't remember when I was last given anything without asking for it.'

She does not intend to be unpleasant. She is no more bitter than usual this evening, only more tired, more harassed. The words came tumbling out, escaping on their own from where they are hidden.

And yet again a fatal little fact has been brought to the light of day, capable of harvesting fresh spite endlessly, fresh thoughts and words. Heavy masses of suppressed resentment are stirring in them both, resentment at all the trifles that pile up through the days and the years, and finally acquire explosive force. A small stone has started to roll, but a small stone can give warning of an avalanche.

It seems to him that what she said was extremely unjust. If there is anything he is sure about, it is that he has always done his duty. More than his duty. She, on the other hand, is unreasonable, silly, childish, petty. Petty, that's the word. If he has behaved badly at any time, it has certainly occurred without his knowledge or intention.

But his wife, who is behaving badly out of bitterness, and knows it very well, cannot think otherwise than that her husband is exactly the same. She assumes forgetfulness to be intentional negligence, and habitual egoism to be willed indifference.

Her mouth has grown small and tense from being closed tight over the things she does not say. But she hides them all in her heart. There they lie, spite piled on spite. She can consult them, and seek nourishment for old resentment whenever she wishes.

So can he. The difference is that he collects essentials, or what he consider to be essentials. He carries a few boulders around, and is holding on to them for the time being: as a man, as a reasonable being, capable of philosophy, of accepting woman as she is and cultivating domestic peace rationally.

She is dragging a burden of pebbles, picked up along the way they have come. Every once in a while one of them slips from her grasp.

A grey existence without end, continual anxious friction, has worn them both down until their souls have become thin and threadbare. Neither of them possesses generosity or lenience any more. And there they sit, one evening among countless others.

He does not answer her immediately. He chews on his pipe, takes it out of the corner of his mouth and puts it back, stretches his legs, rattles his keys in his trouser pocket. Finally he remarks, 'One can hardly say you encourage attentiveness. But let's consider the question. Didn't you get a handbag – a very handsome handbag – when, last summer, wasn't it?'

'It was two years ago, and I had gone on about it for many years before that.'

'Nonsense, it was last summer. I remember it well. Last spring, in fact. Of course I knew you wanted a handbag. I am always told when you think there's something you need,' he adds ironically, loosening what he considers to be a fairly justifiable boulder by way of warning.

She bends her head over her sewing and smiles an evil smile to herself. The things she has mentioned over the years are as nothing by comparison with what has been concealed, what has been borne in bitter silence. She ought to keep silent now as well. But one of those moments has arrived when the whole burden of pebbles threatens to clatter to the ground. There he sits, strong, superior, master of himself and of what he owns, indeed of her and of what she owns as well, in spite of everything that is written and spoken about women's liberation. Only daughters with four children are not liberated. To learn something more, a language, shorthand; to get back her office job and manage with paid help in the house; all have long ago passed beyond the bounds of possibility.

Desperately she tightens her lips, clinging to all that she knows it is wise to cling to. For the sake of the children, for the sake of her own existence. Trifles, taken singly; taken all together, the grey eternity she can never escape except through death. Or except through crazy, impossible actions, such as dividing children, furniture, income, shaking the very foundations. She feels dizzy at the thought. But if she rejects it, she feels a clamp on her chest, a heaviness in her limbs, just as when she has occasionally gone out and must return home again; the reluctance of an organism to obey any longer.

Behind all the trifles lies something big that she cannot put into words. She is not learned, not literary, has no skills in summing up, clarifying, finding precise words that bring order to chaos and give relief. Blindly, as if lost in a thicket, she struggles forward, hurling her pebbles at random.

'And I suppose you haven't had Christmas presents either?' His tone is cold and spiteful.

'Yes, of course. Things for the house, that we would have had to get anyway.'

Out of prudence and for the sake of peace he usually ignores such a reply. Now he decides to speak his mind. There are limits to everything, including a man's patience.

'Sometimes, in fact, pretty often, you express a bitterness that is very wounding,' he begins matter-of-factly. 'I'd like to know what you mean by it. What have you got to accuse me of? Can you say that you have lacked anything for one single day?'

'Not if you're thinking of food and a roof over my head.'

But that's exactly what he is thinking of. It was his duty to provide her with these things, and he has done so, in so far as it was possible. He often had a hard struggle to make ends meet. As for presents? Fancy sitting there talking about presents in the midst of life's struggle, when the ship has often come close to sinking! Only a woman gets that idea. Besides, today she has been given the cactus, a completely superfluous object, sheer luxury for that matter.

'And clothes? Have you lacked clothes?'

'I have had what was absolutely necessary, a mere minimum.'

That stung him. And the sting remained in the wound, remained for ever in one of the average man's most sensitive spots.

The average man swears slowly and fervently, lifts up a chair and sets it down roughly again, demonstrates – in other words, that if he were not in control of himself, heaven help both the living and the dead.

But the stinger resembles other creatures that sting. They sting in what they think is self-defence, and afterwards are helpless, buzzing and hissing aimlessly.

The words stumble over one another as they tumble out of her. The avalanche has begun.

Despairingly she tries to seize and express this reality behind appearances. She fails, and becomes even more excited. Blindly she drags to herself the thoughts that are whirling through her brain, hurling them at him haphazardly.

'The hat,' she shouts. 'The green hat. I've been wearing it for four years. And my winter coat. For *six*. I'm ashamed, I walk along the back streets, I hide from people. But you order a new suit every year for the sake of the office, so that you are treated with respect at the *office*. It doesn't matter how I'm treated where I come and go.'

'Good lord!' he tries to reason, without success.

'A top hat,' she shouts. 'You got yourself a top hat. I suppose that was in order to deceive the office as well.'

'The boss's funeral,' he tries again.

No use. Nothing can stop her now.

'Here I slave away, mending and patching till far into the night, year after year, unable to show myself to people. But it's important to have the cheapest possible wife, like every other necessary household item.' She laughs loudly and shrilly.

Bitter memories stream through her, invitations she did not accept, people to whom she said she was not at home, superior gentlemen and ladies behind counters for whom the badly dressed customer is as the air, the hopeless struggle to build up one's wardrobe after one has come far down in the world and no longer dares to approach these gentlemen and ladies. Out-of-the-way, badly equipped shops, where she searched, anxious and unused to making purchases, among ugly, cheap things for something to brighten up her shabby person. Furtive sneaking in dubious districts to pawn small valuables that could be dispensed with.

And like a grey procession without end, the numbers of evenings spent with the pile of socks, spent longing for the days when, as a young girl, she had an easy office job and carefree living at home, with her own money, pretty clothes, free time, reading, friends, piled up in her body, filling it with a nagging restlessness.

Now she is shouting it all out, shouting confusedly, stammering, stuttering. She weakens her position by sheer unreason. 'A wife. What does it matter how a wife feels? They bury her as cheaply as possible when she's dead and take a new one – a wife . . . a wife – I can't stand any more of it, I can't take it any longer. But you just hum, you think that's exactly how it should be, you go around humming out of tune for years as if nothing was the matter, you stretch across the table instead of asking us to pass you things, you . . .'

'Good lord!' he manages to say once more. She is still shouting, hacking the air in front of her with clenched fists, goaded beyond endurance by the smile on his face.

For now he is smiling mockingly, as do all those who know they are in the right and cannot make themselves heard.

Aversion at the mere sight of him, a feeling resembling nausea, seizes her. There he stands, not in the slightest bit interesting or charming, baggy and slightly sagging at the knees, short-sighted, bald, pot-bellied: an ordinary, boring male like thousands of others. And spiteful. And petty. And dull. *Dull.*

'And I'm married to *you*!' she shouts. 'I have four children by you. God almighty!'

With her hands in front of her face she sobs aloud.

All this female unreason had made him obstinate and calm. He had felt himself grow in stature as he stood there representing good sense, moderation, a clear perspective. His smile had changed from one of scorn to pity. After all, she was making herself totally impossible. He pitied her.

But at her last words, his smile became malicious. 'You should have had a rich husband,' he said icily. 'Your desire for luxury . . .'

But then she laughs loudly and hysterically. 'I have to laugh,' she groans. And laughs again.

She remembers the little collar of black rabbit fur that once held some attraction for her. As if ordered, it comes floating up from what has been half forgotten. Beside it in the furrier's window there hung grey squirrel, blue fox, marten, all the softness and warmth a woman can desire to wrap herself in. It was the black rabbit she dreamt about. Not because it was so special, but because it was attainable, possible to acquire without sacrifice or ruination. She needed it, she froze at the neck, she knew the cold made her ugly and blue; if she managed to get through the Christmas period without extra help it would be paid for. She stopped him in front of the window. He did not, or would not, understand. And winter followed winter.

Luxury! As if she had wanted pearls and Paris fashions! Yet there had been a few years, long ago, when her heart had beat like a child's on all sorts of occasions: on the annual wedding anniversary, even when she heard his step on the stairs. Had he hit on something or other today? Flowers, a book, or – why not? – an unnecessary, slightly frivolous object, that would *last*, would accompany her through the years. A brooch, a ring? A symbol to show that one was worth a little frivolity? It was childish, but she had yearned for it.

That had been the time when she herself had thought up all sorts of things, silly little surprises that were never successful.

The old annual disappointments remain within her like skewers in a piece of meat. He was the kind of man who is forgetful about such things. A long time passed before she taught herself not to expect anything. When he suddenly turned up with the cactus in the middle of the sequence of years on an ordinary working day, she was so astonished that she did not manage to say a word.

Luxury? Yes, after all, the sort of luxury that poor people can enjoy. A little romance, a little caring for one another. It was not necessary to have a gold-mine to pay for it. During their engagement she had thought: he's a shy, reserved type; he'll change. He hadn't.

If only he had said now and again, 'How I wish I could give you such and such!' It would have been enough, more than enough; it would have quieted her distress. If only he had said 'My darling'. But he did not use such words.

For now she sees the reality behind appearances. The flood of words has cleared the way for it. She recognizes her privation. It is dead, it distresses her no longer. And yet she still drags it around, a dead weight that is poisoning her.

And she is ashamed. Ashamed of all the cheap, paltry words she has used of the unspeakable; the stupid, vulgar euphemisms for a simple truth.

'If only you had sometimes said . . .' she sobs.

'Said what?'

'Oh, nothing,' she replies, and is even more ashamed,

crouching lower in her chair, crying quietly.

He is standing, supporting himself on the back of a chair, gripping it tightly. Between two dabs with her handkerchief she sees that an avalanche has started in him as well. It is moving behind his stiff, immobile face, behind his jaw, which seems to her to be broader than before. Fear seeps into her, woman's ancient fear of man, the master, who holds her fate in his hand.

It dawns on her that she has made life even worse for herself. It feels as if she has been forced to do it.

He is silent. She sits sobbing, listening to the silence. It is ringing, pregnant with what is unsaid. Words are so useless; you can never find the right ones. But silence is heavy with meaning.

A bed creaks above them, a child turning over. It increases the impression of imminent destruction. She waits, ill at ease.

When he speaks he says that he will take the necessary initial steps first thing in the morning, and find out what has to be done legally. For the time being he will have to rent a room in town, arrange matters as best he can. For both their sakes, for the children's sakes, so that there will be as little friction as possible in the immediate future. The idea is not new to him, on the contrary. After what she has just said, such a solution ought to be welcome to her as well.

She does not reply. Paralysed by his icy tone of voice she keeps her eyes on his feet pacing the floor: from the corner cupboard to the rocking-chair and back again.

Two households, she is thinking, two households. Now the children won't get to the dentist this year either. Erling has eight visible holes, Arne five. Astrid has complained of toothache as well. And I've almost promised her a new coat for the autumn; at least I promised to talk to Father. The old one can't possibly last another year, it would be a shame if she had to use it. And Gert *must* have shoes.

It is as if the holes in the children's teeth give her toothache in her own. In her mind's eye she sees Astrid going out through the gate in the old coat that is so grotesquely short and has no hem left. She glimpses her husband, bald and a little short-sighted, pot-bellied, alone in a room somewhere in town, a depressingly furnished, cheap room with a disagreeable landlady. A forgotten, hidden feeling, sympathy for him, rises in her, filling her eyes with fresh tears.

He, for his part, is remembering hard work, nights spent on overtime, self-denial; rebellious longing for his bachelor days; or for something new, new women; reluctance to go home. He too is carrying a dead weight, the boyish disappointment of the male with a woman who is not an unchanging vision of beauty like the one he fell in love with.

Somewhat rephrased, he tells her so. Deliberately and with steady aim he slings his boulders at her. Each one hits the target.

A support in life's struggle, an ally, in short a *wife*, he had believed in that once upon a time, however . . .

'I've put up with your capricious moods, your everlasting discontent, your oppressive silence. I could have done what other husbands with peevish wives do, gone out with friends to cafés, gone drinking, but no, I came home, I thought I owed it to you. God knows what it cost me sometimes. I literally had to drag myself up the steps.'

Involuntarily she raises her head. 'You too?' she almost says, but does not.

'As for presents?' he continues. For heaven's sake, it hadn't occurred to him. After all, they were both adults. Like many others he is forgetful about such things. He hasn't had the money, he's had to struggle to obtain the necessities of life, and thought she had understood that. Does she imagine that other husbands in difficult circumstances dance attendance with presents? That reasonable wives demand that sort of thing?

She removes the handkerchief from her face and looks at him in desperation. 'But that's not what I mean.'

'Really?' He pauses.

But when she starts fumbling for different words, he shrugs his shoulders impatiently. 'Fortunately most wives understand that a man has to look respectable when he goes to work, and give the impression of financial reliability.'

He has been *faithful*. She need not look at him so ironically. For a man to be faithful year in and year out is not entirely unimportant.

At that she suddenly feels she can still wound. 'You have neither the money nor the initiative to do anything else. It's not in your character.'

'You know nothing about it,' he remarks calmly, demolishing her completely. And here she is faced with her own limitations. What does a woman know about a man, what does someone bound know about someone who is free? The wide world begins outside the door of the home. He goes out into it every morning and is away until evening.

'I did my best to adapt to you, to teach myself to take you as you were, both for our own and the children's sakes. To tell the truth, I gave up trying long ago.'

Silent, fearful and numb, she is still watching his feet pacing the floor.

He stands still. 'We'll have to reach a settlement as best we can. Where Erling is concerned, I take it for granted that he will stay with me. He's fifteen years old now.'

His words cut into her like knives. Erling is her first-born, her big boy.

They say no more, but sit looking around at what has been their living-room for many years as if they were in a strange place. What had been kept secret has entered their lives. All contours are changed by it.

As long as it remained hidden within them they had, in spite of everything, spun thousands of threads between them: a living web of common striving for everyday existence.

Now it has been torn to shreds, and they are tugging at the threads as if they were exposed nerve ends. Gert will have to give up his violin lessons, she is thinking, the boy's sorrow nagging at her already. Her husband's socks and underwear come into her mind. She will have to take them home once in a while, to see to them. Strangers don't do it satisfactorily.

She imagines the parcel in front of her clearly, knowing how it will feel to send it away, out of the house. And Erling's underwear! She could scream.

No walking holiday with them this year, he is thinking. With the extra expenses I'll be having now I shan't be able to manage it.

The disappointed faces of four children crowd round him.

A miserable feeling of failure, of not having succeeded in doing one's duty, is tearing at them both. As if suddenly awakened from sleep she sees how tired and aged he is. The bent head, the thinning hair, the strained eyes, these are the signs of hard work, of grey everyday existence. Behind it she notices something she thinks she has not seen before: the boy who never quite dies in a man, who always needs consideration, however old he may become. And she remembers that her winter coat and her hat were once really attractive items of clothing, solid and quite expensive.

He, for his part, has noticed during his silent pacing how faded she is as she sits there, a shadow of former times. He observes it in a new way, without irritation, with tenderness. He is thinking that she has really managed very well, after all. And been brave about it.

A timorous desire, a ghost of a longing to stroke his hair, to lay her head on his shoulder as she used to once upon a time, flits through her for an instant. A feeling that, if she did so, all malice would vanish.

A vague idea of putting an arm round her, of turning her face towards his as – well, as he used to long ago – steals through his mind. A notion that then the two of them would immediately come together again.

The bed creaks upstairs.

Inadvertently their eyes meet, and both of them see in the other's a hint of loneliness and helplessness.

But neither of them finds a way out of the dilemma. They have learned to conceal themselves from one another, to say nothing to each other, to shout loudly and bitterly or speak coldly and scornfully about externals; not to understand and to be honest.

'Well, well,' he says calmly, as he gathers up the newspapers, 'We're agreed, then. As I said, I'll see to it tomorrow morning. Tonight I'll sleep here on the divan.'

'As you like,' she answers without expression.

For a moment they look into each other's eyes warily and with hostility.

The Picture from Hull

It is hanging on its own on an otherwise empty wall. It depicts a ship's crew on deck with a solitary woman among all the men. It's behind glass, and framed. A brand new, narrow oak frame.

On the next wall a picture of a child in christening robes, taken by a country photographer. On the third an old-fashioned oleograph above a sofa. Another on the fourth above a sideboard. And then the ship's crew again.

In front of the sofa a round table with a hanging lamp above it. The kind that was made for oil but has a light bulb instead where the glass funnel used to be.

A young woman is busy at the table, laying a cloth, setting out cups, one dish with palely baked macaroon rings from the grocer, another with heavy Danish pastries, moving the dining-chairs about; then she goes across to the ship's crew and adjusts it, even though it was hanging straight. 'Nice we got it up, Sjur. Especially now.'

'Yes, I suppose so,' says Sjur. He is striding up and down, his hands in his trouser pockets and his pipe in the corner of his mouth. Sometimes it looks as if he is about to go over to the picture, but he stops himself and looks out of the window instead. Between fuchsias and geraniums, which are crowded on the sill, can be glimpsed small, poorly kept outhouses, a patch of field, a length of drystone wall, a tethered cow, a few chickens running and pecking. An extremely modest little farm, all in all. And a bend in the country road.

His wife goes and opens the door of the bedroom, places it half open, wide open, half open again, decides on something in between. Beds, a wash-stand and a cradle are standing there close together or wherever there is room, their paint worn, not a pretty sight. But over the bed there is a large crocheted bedspread, white and new and attractive. Finally the door is left ajar so that it can be seen, and not too much of the rest.

In the cradle a baby is lying, gurgling to itself. The mother lifts it out, talks to it, checks to see if it is wet, adjusts its bib. Then she is back at the ship's crew again.

'Leave it alone, Anna. It'll fall down if you go on like that. It's quite all right as it is, in my opinion.'

'Nice to have it on the wall,' says Anna. 'And specially now. Can you see it, little one?' – pointing to direct the baby's attention.

'She's coming!' Two little boys run indoors and throw the door wide open.

And, quite right, a person comes into sight, walking round the bend in the road and shortly afterwards she is standing in the living-room.

She is of a different category from her hosts, prosperous middle class in dress and manner, while Sjur and Anna are poor working class. The difference appears in the fact that she has brought presents, a pretty scarf for Anna, sweets for the children, a packet of cigarettes for Sjur. It lies there, all by itself, at the edge of the table. Twice Anna has said, '. . . and cigarettes for you, Sjur.' 'Uh-huh,' says Sjur. That isn't anything like enough, so Anna has to make up for it.

She talks feverishly as she pours coffee and presses her pale macaroons and indigestible Danish pastry on her guest. She rocks the baby back and forth so that it won't scream, and prevents the boys from hanging over the table. 'Be quiet, Alfred. All right, *take* a cake. Have you said thank you politely, Olaf? You must drink your coffee, Mrs Enersen. And *do* eat, please give me the pleasure. I don't know how often I've told Sjur all these years, we'll never meet anyone kinder than Mrs Enersen. Remember that Christmas Eve, when everything was so dreadful, and Mrs Enersen suddenly turned up!' Anna wipes the mouth of the baby and her own tears that are welling up. 'Haven't I reminded you many times, Sjur?'

'Yes, yes, of course.' Sjur removes the pipe from the corner of his mouth and replaces it again.

The guest gestures away from herself, hoping to keep more emotion at bay. She empties her coffee-cup and looks around her, at the hanging lamp, the sofa and the sideboard, which Sjur and Anna had once set up house with in youthful extravagance and blind faith in the future. The furniture has not propagated. It all looks as out of place and lonely as it has always been.

'We have a bedroom as well,' says Anna, for the sake of the bedspread.

'I see you have. Very nice and attractive.'

'That picture's new.' Anna nods in the direction of the ship's crew. Sjur is on his way towards it.

But all the guest says is 'Oh, is it?' and peers out at the farm through the potted plants. 'Brave of you both to embark on this.'

Sjur swerves across to the window side, having nothing really against this topic either. 'I got it on reasonable terms,' he says, clearly the sort of fellow who has always had something to fall back on in spite of unemployment and other problems. He leaves it to his guest to decide how he can have acquired the property, merely explaining, 'It's not a large farm, but the position is good.'

'I'm sure,' says the stranger, without curiosity but full of admiration for enterprising people.

'So we have our own milk,' continues Anna. 'Milk and eggs and potatoes and fresh air for the children. That means a lot. If only Sjur gets the time, we'll have a garden as well. We have a couple of rows of carrots already, he lifted them for me last year. But I'll have a few flowers in time, marigolds and suchlike if nothing else, enough to take in a bunch on Sundays. And chives and parsley. You can't have everything at once.' She smiles apologetically. 'Sjur's had so much to put in order.'

'Quite a bit to mend, yes,' Sjur gestures with his pipe towards the outhouses, where an occasional unpainted plank in the sleazy walls, an occasional new tile, are witness to his activity.

'Oh yes, yes.' Their guest nods understandingly, without

seeming to come to any conclusions regarding Sjur's activity; that, for example, it might have extended as far as those flowerbeds. If *that* was what Anna was afraid of.

She gets to her feet, takes down the child in the christening robe, and hands it across the table. 'That's our Lily. I often said to Sjur, imagine, Mrs Enersen was never to see our Lily. She was on the way when you moved, you and your family. And since then. . . .'

The guest looks at the picture, in the way one looks at dead persons one has never known, with polite sadness. 'What a good one. What was the matter with her?'

'Diphtheria.' And Anna embarks on the story of Lily's illness, the suffocating attack in the middle of the night, Sjur having to fly to the telephone, and what the doctor said and what Sister at the hospital said and why Lily couldn't be saved. No resistance, rickets in an advanced stage. Mrs Enersen can surely see that she wasn't a strong child. You can see that from the picture . . .

'Maybe . . . but a good picture all the same,' the guest assures her sympathetically.

Anna hangs Lily back on the wall and is on her way towards the ship's crew again but remembers her duties as hostess. 'And you, Mrs Enersen? And the children? And your husband? You're all comfortable?'

The guest's tone alters. 'I'm not called Mrs Enersen any more. I've taken back my maiden name and call myself Berg. We've been divorced for a couple of years already, Mr Enersen and I.'

Sjur stops pacing about the floor. Both he and Anna look stupid.

'No, you can't mean it!' exclaims Anna finally. Sjur makes no comment. Lost in thought he has resumed his pacing.

Mrs Enersen Berg pushes her cup away and plays with the teaspoon, looking down at it. 'Yes . . . that's how it goes. Mr Enersen has married again. I think I am fortunate as I am. The children are with me. I've started a small business in my home town, and it doesn't do too badly. I'm in this area to arrange business contacts. I don't suppose we'd have met each other again otherwise.' She looks up, her expression satisfied and youthful, well dressed and confident. She's in no difficulty.

'No,' says Anna. 'I couldn't believe my own eyes yesterday, down on the road.' She still doesn't seem to believe them. She opens them wide and adds, 'And here you are, divorced. And we, who thought . . . who didn't know any better. . . .'

Sjur halts and pokes at his pipe impatiently. He coughs warningly.

'We were both of us restrained,' says Mrs Enersen Berg. 'But that doesn't mean that people are suited to each other.'

'No, no,' from Sjur.

And he resolutely joins in the conversation, until it becomes stranded in tactlessness and incomprehension. He positions himself at the window and points at the piece of earth below with his pipe.

'Come and look at this, Mrs Berg. Last year I harvested from that ditch and over to the drystone wall. Oats.'

'Oh, really?' Mrs Berg takes up her position by the window, following his gestures and looking as knowledgeable as she can.

But Anna remains seated for a good while, rocking the baby, staring straight in front of her with a strained and concentrated expression.

Mrs Berg says she must go. Then Anna says recklessly, 'There's no need to take the ferry. Sjur can row you across.'

For Sjur must do something. He hasn't thanked her for the cigarettes, making as if he hasn't even seen them. The fact painfully embarrasses Anna.

'Boat's lying waterlogged,' Sjur informs them coolly. 'We'll have to get wet.' He is standing leaning one elbow on the sideboard, looking down at his long legs, examining them from every angle as if to judge how things will go. 'If only I had a pair of waders.'

'Waterlogged? For heaven's sake!'

'I told you, it's waterlogged.'

Mrs Berg spreads out her hands. 'Of course there's no need for a farmer to break off in the middle of the working day. I'll manage, I'm sure.'

'Have you anything to do at the moment, Sjur?'

'There's always something to do on a farm,' says Mrs Berg placatingly.

But Anna gets up, crosses the floor and takes the ship's crew down from the wall.

'Look at this, Mrs Ener . . . I mean Mrs Berg. Here's Sjur that time he was at sea. There he is.'

She points at a young man standing among the others, Sjur in his heyday, tall, dark, a cigarette at the corner of his mouth and cloth cap askew. A swell fellow, a danger to impressionable hearts, terribly dangerous to Anna once upon a time. He stands at ease, his hands in his trouser pockets and his shirt open far down his chest.

'That's the waitress.' Anna points to the solid, well-built woman standing alone among the men. With a defiant smile in her strong face she is standing beside Sjur, her hand on his shoulder.

'It was that time,' volunteers Sjur. 'It was in Hull. A photographer came on board one day.'

'Oh, really?' says Mrs Berg.

'I just wanted to show it to you. We didn't have it on the wall before, we've just had it framed.' Anna hangs the picture carefully back in position, taking care that it's not crooked. 'Nice to have it,' she remarks.

Mrs Berg suddenly moves nearer, looks at it closely and says, 'How handsome you were then! How good it is of you!'

'Hm,' says Sjur, and smiles with becoming modesty. In fact, he bows as well, and apologizes for the fact that the boat happens to be waterlogged today. He stands on the step while Anna, the baby on her arm and the boys in tow, accompanies her to the gate.

Mrs Berg disappears round the bend in the road.

Sjur is busy poking his pipe when Anna comes back into the house. He is looking thoughtful.

'Didn't you *see* the cigarettes she gave you?' Anna cannot let the embarrassing topic alone. There are others burning inside her, but this one drops out first. Never mind about the boat being waterlogged, though it's contrary to all usual practice. But that Sjur shouldn't so much as thank her . . .

'Of course I saw them. There they are, lying on the table.'

'Couldn't you have thanked her then, Sjur?'

'Didn't I say thank you? Surely I did?'

'No.'

'Then I didn't say thank you.' Sjur has finished his poking, presses down the tobacco and lights it. 'Besides, I can buy my own cigarettes if I want to.'

Anna is silenced, but only for a moment. 'It was a kindness all the same. And what about that Christmas when things were so bad, and she brought us food and clothes for the children. Alfred had just been born. I shall never forget how good it was to have proper nappies for him, poor little thing. You don't remember that, do you, Alfred?'

'Do you want him to remember when he was just born?' asks Sjur. 'What nonsense!'

'I mean . . .'

'You mean!' Sjur strides up and down. 'As if she had any problems giving away those nappies!'

'But what about the food, Sjur? And five kroner for Alfred's savings bank, and . . .'

'Well, and was that so difficult? The way they were placed? Things weren't so bad with us either, but you carried on so.'

'Carried on? Their maid was up in the attic and saw the snow lying on our window-sills. I had come home the same day and had had Alfred and could scarcely stand. Because he arrived early, three weeks early. I had nothing ready, not even the nappies. I hadn't even so much as a piece of material to sew. You'd been without work for thirteen months . . .'

'Oh!' Sjur squirms. 'I'm sick of your moaning. We weren't so badly off. It wasn't my fault that the snow came in. The landlord wouldn't do any repairs, so . . .'

'Of course it wasn't *your* fault! The maid ran straight down and said, Oh God, they haven't even enough warmth to melt the snow off the window-sills in the attic. Have I said it was your fault?'

'I always have to be told that it was like this and it was like that. We were *all right*. You've never lacked for anything, neither you nor the kids. I'm not the only one to have been without work for a while.'

'I only meant that Mrs Ener . . . Mrs Berg was *kind.*'

'Oh!'

Sjur continues to turn something over in his mind, a counter-attack. And it comes.

'You're sitting wondering about this divorce. As if it was something unusual, a divorce!'

'Not unusual. . . .' Anna wipes the baby's nose. 'It was just that they looked happy together.'

'Did they have to *be* happy because of that?' Sjur halts, furious at this simple method of reaching conclusions. 'They *didn't* suit each other, didn't you hear?'

'I talked to the maid every day. She never said she'd heard one angry word,' insists the incorrigible Anna.

'Silly woman!'

The baby whimpers, wet and unhappy. Anna has forgotten that she had been sitting full of anxiety, feeling the moisture seep in to her own body, and thinking that she would change her blouse and everything else, if only Mrs Berg would leave. While the whimpering gradually changes to loud screaming, she continues rocking the bundle pointlessly. Helplessly she contemplates something she cannot understand, which seems to be so simple and obvious to Sjur.

'She looked as if she was all right too. I don't understand . . . start a business? You need to have money for that. Has Enersen given it her, do you think?'

'Shouldn't think so' is Sjur's opinion. He is standing with his head thrown back, contemplating the matter from his point of view. 'Great lady,' he declares. 'Great lady.'

'And him married again, too. My goodness!'

'Is *that* so strange? That a man should marry again? A man of his age?'

'No – if they're divorced already, I suppose. . . .' Suddenly there are tears in Anna's voice. It will not be long before she is crying.

'That's probably why they got divorced. So that he could marry someone else.' Sjur's voice is not choked with tears. It resembles more that of an impudent boy, daring to see how far he can go.

'Oh, surely not!' exclaims Anna involuntarily.

'Well. . . .' Sjur gazes at his shoes again, examines them carefully, from the front, from the back, from the sides. 'Maybe he knew somebody he thought he could be happier with . . .'

'Happier?' In astonishment, Anna repeats Sjur's word and sits pondering it. Do people think like that? The days pass, and the years, children come, one after the other. Happy? Happier? Is there time to think like that? One is just glad when things go well.

But Sjur is standing in front of the picture from Hull. His pipe is puffing, he is flexing his knees. Now he's the one taking the trouble to see that it's hanging straight, this piece of evidence of what sort of a fellow he is, when all's said and done.

Good lord! Sjur feels he still recognizes himself as he was then. From old habit he presses his tongue against his teeth – two missing in the middle of the upper jaw; strokes his hair along the crown of his head – not much on top there either. But that's not what it takes, a couple of teeth or a little hair more or less, not for a man.

And he turns, still standing with lifted chin, resolute mouth and distant gaze; as if surrounded by wide horizons and an irresponsible bachelor life, by strange harbours and changing adventures he stands there with nothing of the small farmer with a brood of children about him. In different circumstances Anna would have watched him warmly and with approval. And proudly and lovingly and recklessly. . . .

Now the sight only makes her feel anxious, together with a sudden resentment against the picture from Hull. It surfaces as if she has been carrying it round without knowing it. And she has insisted that it should go up on the wall, be shown, yet she has hated it every time she found it in the drawer where it lay. Understand that, if you can. Anna does not.

That waitress, who probably isn't dead at all, who may still be at sea, doesn't she seem like an eternal threat to Anna's uncertain and laborious world? She and her equals, the unencumbered and the free, the ones without children and drudgery?

Anna is the last to know what she really has in mind, as she strides across to the picture. But she stands squarely in front of it and mutters unconsciously, 'Oh no . . . pity to spoil the frame, I suppose. . . .'

Then she gives it a shove so that it hangs thoroughly crooked.

And does what the waitress would never have done: sits down and cries.

The Women in the Bath-house

When the new girl came to the bath-house for the first time, she stood fiddling with the buckle of her belt and looking about her as if she didn't know what to make of it. She was very young with huge eyes, from somewhere up in the mountains, where they lived in small, low houses with flat roofs and things were quite different. There was a cackle of voices. Loud splashing from somewhere. Farther on inside someone was singing. The air was heavy with steam and fragrance. The female slaves ran about, getting in each other's way, grumbling to each other under their breath as they passed. The black marble slabs were bulging with naked female flesh.

The new girl had never imagined that it could occur in such bulk. She realized that it was the older wives who swelled up like this, and thought, appalled, you can get like that, you can get like that. It made her feel great fear and repugnance, for she loved the supple slenderness of her limbs, her light, small body, the give in her walk. She hid her face in the crook of her arm and said to herself, I shan't, I shan't. At home in the mountains they became dry as trees with the years, as if baked by work and sun. It seemed to her to be more decent, more right.

She turned away and looked upwards at the curved vaults. They stood, held up by clustered columns, the one traced into the other in perspective as they receded, looking as if they were hovering over the steam and the noise. They were as splendid as in a mosque, encrusted with mosaics. Lamps in finely wrought chains hung from them and shone dully, moisture on the surface of the glass.

She looked down at the floor. Mosaic there as well between beautifully positioned tiles. It was enough to make one fall to one's knees, forehead to the floor. But that was impossible with the crowd and the noise.

She heard a splash through all the other splashes and looked about her dazedly for the sound. In a large pool something unimaginable was happening. A huge white female body, far whiter than was natural, was struggling through the water on her back. Long yellow hair, yellow as corn or honey, floated about her, her arms were working like paddles. The new girl had never seen anything so large and white and yellow before. The exaggeratedly light colours struck her as obscene. When the woman suddenly turned over on her stomach, landed at the steps and grew with every step she took, her hair like a wet, ragged, yellow fur around her body to far down her thighs, the new girl hid her face in her arm again, retreated backwards and refused to look any more.

She heard the woman laugh and say something she did not understand.

The wives would meet in the baths. The oldest and fattest of them had begun to suffer from their obesity. They were scant of breath and had pains here and there and in their legs. But they wanted to be like the younger ones. So they sighed and groaned, stuffed chocolates in their mouths and insisted on being massaged. 'Harder!' they shouted. The slaves massaged them until the sweat ran off them and they turned red in the face from their exertions.

Some of the slaves were older than the others, were born here, and knew all about the place. They kept order. If there was any trouble or fuss, it was always among the slaves who came from far away. They might suddenly become perverse and dejected, getting weak in the arms and not massaging hard enough for the fat wives; now and then they even lay down and sulked, holding their hearts, unable to manage any more. The oldest of them all would have to intervene and rebuke them. Occasionally she might have to report to the eunuch outside, and the rebel would be led away for punishment. But not often. On the whole the oldest slave was looked upon as a reasonable and pleasant person.

Many of the slaves spoke candidly and frankly. They could well afford to do so, efficient and indispensable as they were. Those who could massage really forcefully and without visible effort could say almost whatever they liked.

Outside the door the chief eunuch paced up and down. He, too, had become more outspoken as time passed, as a result of his holding a position of trust. He, too, expressed his opinion to certain people, but did so, as it were, with discrimination. It was not a good sign to be browbeaten by him; it might mean that one's star was seriously in decline, or it might even be a hint of the silken cord and of death. He was in favour in the highest places, and knew everything, it was said. Most people were terrified of him.

Shaken and embarrassed the new girl went to the bath-house every day. After all, she had to get used to what could not be otherwise. Time began to pass, for her as for the rest of them. She was reserved, not at all the type who can throw her weight about and is automatically listened to. There was nothing unusual about her. She was over-large, like most young women of her tribe, with almond-shaped, gazelle-like eyes, over-full lips, a snub nose with sensitive nostrils, a tiny ring in the side of the nose, and tattooing on her forehead and chin. Ordinary. She had been brought into the harem more out of prudence than anything else. Because she might be good to turn to one day. One never knew.

For a long time she kept to herself, preferring to be as unnoticed as possible. But there was a foolish girl there, a girl from another country, who could say a few incomprehensible words only with difficulty, and didn't understand the simplest rules of make-up and dress. The new girl sought her company because she seemed so kind and harmless and never laughed at anyone or was nasty to them. They scarcely talked to one another, just kept beside each other and smiled at one another now and again. One day a slave said to the foolish girl, 'Come before the face of the master? You may never get there in all your life. There are plenty who live and die here without having even seen him, and you. . . .'

That was all.

But the foolish girl began to whimper. Once a fool, always a fool. The new girl tried to comfort her, but all she got for an answer was 'I'm so unhappy'. It was impossible to get anything more out of her, except that she never slept at night.

Among the older wives were some who enjoyed talking over their memories. They did so loudly, so that everyone could hear. 'When I think how he loved the song of the nightingale,' they might say. 'We lay there often, listening to them until dawn.'

'And the fountain,' said another. 'That quiet plashing, that slight rippling. . . .'

They agreed on many things, and mostly they were well reconciled. But they looked askance at the young ones and at the young ones' slaves who were never dejected. They called to their own that, if they were not massaged as they ought to be, then God have mercy on them all.

In the middle of the bath-house stand the scales. When using them some shriek and laugh and behave like young girls, although they are far from being so. They are the ones who have never been before the face of the master. And never will either, say the plain-speaking slaves, sneering contemptuously at this as at so much else.

Those who are beginning to be really old, who flush uncontrollably and have started to feel too warm in and out of season, have their secrets. The chocolates they eat are not ordinary chocolates. They are brought by an old woman, who is led heavily veiled along back alleys to the palace. The slaves giggle, and the oldest wives of all, who have white hair and no teeth and have become quite passive, say, 'Poor things.'

Mares' secretions, it is whispered. It's supposed to relieve the drawbacks of ageing, keep it at bay. The new girl blushed on behalf of her sex when she heard it, and felt nauseated.

Women, women, women. They treated each other as women do. They interrupted each other the whole time, never allowing the other to finish what she had to say. They cast quick, watchful little glances sideways at each other and smiled sweetly the next minute. No sooner had they turned their backs on each other than they gossiped to the first passer-by. Many of them were what one calls best friends.

In the mountains you saw, not just women, but men as well. They walked to and fro between the houses, had serious matters to discuss, arrived on horseback, rode away, sat in the shade, met for consultation. They helped with the gardens, with the irrigation systems. Always something important.

Here there wasn't a man to be seen. Only the eunuch.

She learned much about women. One was that when they took their clothes off they could become amazingly bold in their movements and in other ways. How they sang! They hurled the notes out. The resonance in the bath-house gave them great courage.

Some caressed one another, kissing and fondling each other, lying with their heads in one another's laps, gazing deeply and intensely into each other's eyes. The oldest said of them, too, 'Poor things!' *They* had lived life to the full and could afford a little pity.

A number of the women had children with them, some of them boys who had not yet reached the age when they were to be fostered among men. Sometimes they fought and screamed, and a great tumult would result. Excited young mothers were drawn into the quarrel and had to be separated too. They formed factions, and it took time to calm them down again. The episode would be gossiped about for days afterwards.

Only occasionally did there occur a sudden, almost surprised silence. All the women looked at each other and smiled self-consciously. The rippling of the small fountain in the middle of the pool could be heard clearly, a quiet, pleasant little sound, making one even more homesick.

Time passed and the new girl was new no longer. She was one of those who had been there a good while. She watched others being brought in and becoming the new ones. Once she went over to a girl who looked as if she might be from one of the neighbouring tribes in the mountains. But the girl needed no comfort. She said, 'It's clearly important to keep in the forefront here.' And went boldly to join the others.

One morning the foolish little girl had died of her unhappiness. People generally don't believe it, but foolish little girls can die of it. She lay there, her snub nose tilted upwards, the mourners sitting beside her. Many who had never given her a thought, let alone a word, went into her room to look at her, to join in the weeping for a while, to sigh, and go again.

At sunset she was carried out to be buried.

A tall, pale, quiet girl with red hair stood out from the others. She did nothing to win the slaves' favours as so many of the other young ones did, keeping herself to herself, talking to no one. Some of them said she didn't know the language, others that she was arrogant and in addition came from an utterly barbaric country where the women were allowed to go free and behaved beyond the limits of decency. She would not even be massaged, but bathed herself with her own hands and kept everyone at arm's length.

One day when both of them chanced to be standing a little to one side, she suddenly said to the girl from the mountains, 'In my country women are not shut away, in my country they go where they like, and many of them *do* as they like.'

'They are not shut away in my home either.'

'Do they do as they like?'

'Ye-es. At any rate they like doing what they do.'

'That's not the same. But never mind, many of them don't want things to be otherwise. Here we may be forced to do what we don't like. But he's not going to get me, I shall scratch his face, I'll climb over the wall one night and run away.'

The girl from the mountains began to tremble throughout

her body. What sort of words and thoughts were these? Did one do things like that? Would one dare to do it? Didn't she know that the walls were many and high, and that if she were caught, and she would be caught, the executioner would come at once with his curved sword? If you used your ears you picked up gossip about such escapades and how they would end. Tales were still told about them, even though they happened long ago.

'The master is good to those who please him,' she said timidly. 'Everyone says so.'

The other snorted. 'Good? An old sensualist. A disgusting old man, cruel when it suits him.'

The girl from the mountains crept away. It was safest to be at a distance from such dangerous talk.

But she did not forget it.

In the evenings she stood on tiptoe at her barred window, looked out through the grating, and knew painfully well where life would lead her.

Like the others in her village she could have gone down to the entertainment quarter in the nearest town, earned her dowry, come home again, and married. She could have come back with her belt full of clinking coins, for the strangers from far away like being with girls of her tribe, and pay well. She could have had several men to choose from, would have had one that she liked, perhaps, young like herself, and handsome. She recalls the neighbours' boys she used to play with, and thinks of them with longing.

She could have had children, heavy jewellery, beautiful carpets, could have received guests, could have stood at the well in the evenings chatting to the other women, could have gone home, calm and dignified, with the water-jar on her head, her silver chains tinkling as she walked, her heavy earrings swinging slowly to and fro.

She could have worked in the fresh air in the garden, helped with the olive and date harvest, could have stood with a basket at the foot of a ladder, being handed the fruit, while a young man smiled at her from above. And gone in to market the next morning, before the air was too hot, the little donkey on its spindly legs staggering under its load of flowers and fruit.

Things she had never thought about before come into her mind: the scarcely heard trickle of the tiny, almost invisible streams before they had collected neatly in the wide ditch and run purling along it, the entire well-planned irrigation system with its life-giving freshness, its clear little pools. The donkey pulling a wheel with jars that disperse the water, up with the full jars from one side, down with them so they can be emptied on the other, the donkey with a bandage over its eyes, plodding and plodding for hours on end, the creaking of leather straps, of ropes and of wood.

She fingers her tattoos, the one on her forehead, the one on her chin. Neither of them has had the power to protect her. When the palace bid for her, she had thought she was coming to far greater honour and happiness than her sisters who, one after the other, went down to the town and earned their dowries there. She had come to a prison. Perhaps she would remain in it without a husband. That can happen here, she knows that now.

The master of the palace is not young. On the contrary, he is fat and old. But he is powerful, he is rich. He is also good to those in whom he takes pleasure. To dance for him on the palace roof in the evening is great good fortune, say all who have experienced it.

And those in whom he takes no pleasure. . . ? Those to whom he never offers a thought, never asks for, is not even aware he owns? Those purchases the eunuch never tells him about?

A sensualist? Cruel?

The view from the village towards the gardens on the hillside, with the snow-clad mountains behind, comes into her mind so clearly that she thinks she really is seeing it. You can live your life without seeing something properly, until it is lost for ever. Palms and agaves stood out in silhouette against the blue of the range. At night the mountains talked to one another, for mountains have life like everything else, even though they look dead. At midsummer the flames of the bonfires rose towards the sky, and the men leaped over them, above the licking flames. Afterwards they all bathed, young and old, men and women, in the brook, for both fire and water release you from evil and are cleansing.

All this was ordinary, it was life, it happened over and over again. One grew up with it, without noticing that it existed.

But around the palace nothing seems to live, everything is bound hand and foot, holding out as best it can.

The girl with red hair says, 'In my country they throw people into caves when they take their freedom away from them. They don't try to pretend nothing has happened. Here the prisons are more splendid than castles or temples. We haven't anything so magnificent. Yet I'd pull it all down if my hands were strong enough. Oh, if the men from my country could come here, they wouldn't leave one stone upon another. And they'll come.'

'How did you come here?' asks the girl from the mountains, trembling.

'Pirates captured me. That's how I came here.'

And she leaves her again. She always leaves. But in order to leave, one must first have come.

The mountain girl goes away in order to continue dreaming about the loom standing in the shade outside the house. The light-coloured rugs of natural wool with a dark pattern of squares were made on it, and the shawls, the tunics and capes, the wall hangings and donkeys' blankets, simple, warm, indestructible things that seem to her now to be far more valuable than the costly silks from the East which she sees around her and which she is wrapped in herself. Nobody wears wool here.

Her longing will choke her.

The houses were terraced, one above the other, with flat roofs. From them you could talk to women standing in the doorway of the next layer.

The men would collect at the foot of the town wall in their leisure hours, squatting, and shading their eyes with their hands, for the light is strong in the daytime even in the shade, while they discussed all the things men do discuss: horses, trading, farming, war, revenge. Or they listened to the men who could tell them of past events, or of all the strange things that exist between heaven and earth; about the sway-backed woman, about the spirits, the evil ones and the good ones. Her father and her brothers had been sitting there the day the buyer from the palace came by.

She could have been sent in to the travellers who sometimes rested in the village and wanted company for the night, could have returned to her father's house in the morning with a gold coin in her headscarf, she like others. She had been old enough, even though it had perhaps been a little early for her to go down to the town and earn her dowry.

She had danced for joy when they bid for her, she had been proud. Imagine, the palace!

Allie

I have never owned a dog. This omission seems to be almost a flaw in my character. Most people are more fond of dogs than of other animals. Perhaps subconsciously I have been afraid that a dog would claim too much of my attention. Life has brought a few of them in my direction. Fleetingly and superficially I have known Boris, Foggy, Fullstop, Solo and Tell. I also knew Allie fleetingly. When nevertheless I paint her portrait in a few strokes, I do so because of her endearing coquetry, her ingratiating good humour.

On the shores of the Baltic one of our friends has a garden, a garden just as gardens ought to be. Close to the house walls are flower-beds, no bigger than can be watered in a dry period without its getting too much for you. In addition a velvety green lawn, even and thick as a carpet right down to the beach; the kind of lawn that can stand being trodden on, where nobody cries at once 'Don't walk on the grass!' if you so much as set foot on it.

Beyond the lawn, apple trees. Many apple trees. At the time of year when I sat out in the garden daily with my typewriter they were laden with apples, which reddened with every day that passed.

Under the trees a little dog ran about, a little pen-wiper of a black Scottie. Lacking anything else, she ran after birds, her own tail, or things that were invisible to the rest of us. But she preferred to run after stones and sticks which we threw for her. She had her private, crooked branch which hung on a peg in the entrance hall. When we brought it Allie leaped high into the air with delight. What fun, now we were going to play!

To begin with I ignored Allie. As time goes by you become a little cautious about making new àcquaintances, whether animal or human. You know too well what it means to be parted from those you have become fond of. I also lacked experience of dogs, and saw no reason to pay much attention to this one. We were not going to spend much time together.

But Allie did not like being ignored. She would not rest until this new human was properly initiated into the circle, as family member and friend. From the very beginning she danced around me, looked up at me, wagged her tail, and tried to seduce me with two coal-black, shining eyes, full of enthusiasm and friendliness. When they did not seem to make any impression, Allie took the offensive.

It happened from behind. If I sat down on a chair or a sofa, it would not be long before something leaped at my back and thoroughly rumpled my hair. It happened over and over again. Until I gave in, took Allie on my lap, and behaved as the others did towards her. After that she attacked me only now and again when she considered that there should be an end of thinking about irrelevant matters. Amongst other things, Allie was a decided opponent of newspapers, as well as of other forms of reading.

Nobody managed to be seriously irritated by her. We just pretended every now and again; to set an example, and to demonstrate, to ourselves at least, that we were not slaves.

Before we went to bed for the night Allie had to go out, like all well-brought-up dogs, and perform. Our friend would pick her up and put her down outside, in the ring of light from the open door. It is not so easy for the rest of us to do such things on order, and all of us doubtless understood Allie when she immediately began scurrying about on the lawn, sniffing busily at this and that, treating the whole thing as a walk for a walk's sake.

On the other hand the evenings were already getting cold. Her owner wanted to return to the light and the warmth. We could hear him saying 'Hurry up and get on with it, you good-for-nothing beast.' That meant in free, but absolutely correct, translation: 'Darling, delightful little dog, whom I love so much that I have to hide it at all costs, can't you try to see if you can do it?'

Finally Allie did manage to do it, was carried in again, and put to bed in her basket in the kitchen passage. She went round herself in circles and whimpered before she settled down. She would have preferred, just like a child, to be up as long as the grown-ups. At the same time she was sleepy after the toil of the day. She would fall asleep quickly, as children do. Soon we heard her yapping in her dreams.

Allie was in fact only a child. It was her first year of life. Her coat was curly, or rather wavy, not bristly as are those of elderly Scotties. She had all the charm of youth outwardly as well, and was, in all respects, a little lady.

In the morning her task was to activate us with the branch; to get us to finish breakfast, the newspaper, our empty, meaningless (to a dog's ear) barking at each other across the table, and come out to exhilarating, meaningful play on the lawn. Or to a sensible walk in the woods and fields, where thousands of things needed to be sniffed at and investigated.

Her means of persuasion were tail-wagging, dancing around us, jumping up in our faces, eager, shining eyes and little barks. Somewhat despairingly one or other of us would get to his feet and go with her. 'Oh, that dog!' A truly slavish exclamation, even when one finally gives in.

After playing for a while the human would often show signs of flagging interest. Then Allie would introduce a new angle by starting to tease. Or rather, by making you look a fool. She begged, she wagged her tail, the branch was thrown. Allie sprang about half the distance, and then stood panting with malicious pleasure, while the innocent human went to fetch the plaything himself. It was a pricelessly funny sight for a little dog, enough to make her leap high in the air.

Sometimes Allie was the first to tire. She showed it by becoming distracted, suddenly remembering things in the vicinity that had to be sniffed at. She paid no attention to the branch any more, failing even to see it. And before you could count to three, she was somewhere else, enthusiastically busy with urgent matters, to the great relief of the slave, who had been wondering how he was going to get out of it politely this time.

Allie was only a summer dog, that was the tragedy of it. Refugees in time of war* cannot settle down with animals permanently; they know far too little about the future and live mostly in boarding-houses. My friend, like many others, was a refugee, even though he owned a summer place in Sweden. When we returned to Stockholm in the autumn Allie would have to stay behind.

But the person who adopts a pet for the summer does not know what he is doing.

It was no comfort that she would be going back to her birthplace, her mother, her father, the puppies among which she belonged, and her original owner; for he announced that if he did not find a buyer for Allie very soon, he would destroy Allie and her family as well. He had no wish to go on feeding so many dogs, since food had become so scarce and expensive.

What did he want for Allie?

He mentioned what was, in the circumstances, a large amount.

But supposing someone managed to find a person who perhaps could not pay so much, but would be kind to Allie?

No, Allie was a pure-bred, a fine dog, an expensive dog. Either she would be sold for her full value, or . . .

But rather than destroy her?

No, if she could not go to people he knew (this meant my friend), she must go to people who could pay. It was the only

* The Second World War, when Norway was occupied by Germany, and many Norwegians had fled to Sweden.

guarantee that she would be treated properly.

A reasonable argument. The man must have meant kind, honest people and thought that money made them so. Some people do think that, even in this day and age. He would not budge. There followed an anxious time.

It was the most difficult year of the war so far as food supplies in Sweden were concerned. Rations decreased, prices rose, certain foodstuffs such as fish disappeared from the market. There was no privation, compared with the situation in other countries. But anxious souls thought that hunger was not far off in Sweden either. Nobody wanted to buy a dog at all, let alone an expensive dog.

Letters were sent hither and thither. It was a question of Allie's life. We realized that the intention was to pressure my friend into taking her. He did not give in, for it was impossible for him to do so.

The day Allie was taken away and, trustingly wagging her tail, accompanied her hard taskmaster up the hill, was a painful one. She had done this many times before, and probably thought she was going on a pleasant little trip home.

We were leaving. We stood surrounded by suitcases that had already been carried out of the house, and watched her funny little legs trot quickly away beneath the black, curly-haired little body, and heard Allie's happy bark.

Thoroughly honest and guileless as she was herself, she suspected no danger, but went in complete good faith. We knew she would make a fuss about staying the night, knew that if she was shut in she would whimper and become anxious. And perhaps come running here the next day, and sniff in vain round an empty, locked house for her good summer friends.

It was not a pleasant thought. My friend attempted to joke about it all, but he fooled nobody.

Later, sad reports arrived about Allie. She was accused of having stolen chickens, even a whole hen. It was unbelievable.

It couldn't be anything else but falsehood, propaganda, and a threat that the end was not far away. Or a sign that Allie, driven by hunger, had begun to go hunting on her own account. Allie, who had never wanted to be anything but friends with everyone and everything.

Except cows. They terrified her.

Still more letters were dispatched. It looked hopeless. We lived in daily anxiety for Allie's fate, when rescue was suddenly and unexpectedly offered by the British diplomatic corps.

The story of Allie had spread far and wide. One day it reached the British legation in Stockholm, with the result that one of the staff volunteered to buy Allie. He lived outside the city, and did not try to bargain over the price.

Most people in England are fond of animals, and nothing could have been better than that Allie should live in the country, born a country dog as she was. In other words, things brightened up. Now all that had to be done was to get Allie to Stockholm.

That wasn't quite so simple. The journey from Blekinge takes a whole, long day. Allie had to face it alone, shut in a crate in a dark luggage-van. It could not possibly be a pleasant journey for a small dog which was used to running around in woods and fields, and which had no notion of what it was all about.

'Allie will sleep,' said my friend, to comfort himself and others the day Allie was travelling. Still, he fooled nobody. We knew very well that Allie was whimpering – no, crying – that she was suffering from the immobility and the darkness, that she desperately regretted having allowed herself to be stowed away in the crate. One did not need much imagination to see it all.

I was not there when she arrived late in the evening and was met at the station. I only know that she was given water on the way by kind railway staff, and that she was very confused.

She became even more confused when she was urged to perform on the way to the boarding-house. Where was she to do *that*? No grass anywhere. Nothing but stone, noise and clatter. She was also on a lead for the first time in her life.

That Allie finally did what she was supposed to do on a hard, unfriendly pavement was, in my opinion, a noble and indulgent action, taking everything into account from Allie's point of view.

Only when she came in to the room in the boarding-house did she seem to recognize her summer friends properly, and show she was glad to see them, leaping up and wagging her tail.

I met her the following day. She sniffed at me in friendly fashion but remarkably absent-mindedly. Not once did she leap at my back and rumple my hair. With a confused expression she walked at the end of the lead, and only once did I see her looking energetic and happy. It was when we passed a park with green lawns. Then Allie tugged at the lead with all her might, wanting to go there.

She did go there too, but had to be carried away from it forcibly. The green slopes were familiar and dear to her, a fixed point in the middle of all the confusion, an escape.

That same evening Allie disappeared.

It happened out in town, I forget where. I was not there, but was simply phoned and told that Allie was lost alone in the city, an area that was to her completely foreign and vast in size, where the scent of so many people mingled together that a little dog from the country could not possibly be expected to keep track of the couple of humans she knew.

It was heart-rending to think of her wandering about, searching, hungry, thirsty, tired and in despair; or to think that she had been stolen, and was perhaps already locked up in the display window of a pet shop, and would end up with goodness knows whom.

The agreement was that the Englishman was to fetch her the following morning. That was not a pleasant thought either.

The police were informed and given Allie's description: Scotch terrier, young, black, answers to the name of Allie. A similar advertisement was telephoned to a newspaper. There was nothing more to be done. One could only sit down, grieve, hope and wait for what the morning would bring.

We really neither hoped nor waited. We merely grieved.

We didn't know Allie.

Early the next morning a small, black pen-wiper tried to enter the house at No. 7 Strand Street, Stockholm. Fortunately the first person who turned up knew that Allie was lost and let her in.

Then the pen-wiper wanted to go into the lift, for that was where the scent led. She had never used the stairs, neither had her summer friends. Not until the eighth floor did she demand to be let out of the lift, went to one of the doors on the landing, and wagged her tail expectantly. If she had been able to reach the bell, she would probably have rung. But that was, after all, beyond the bounds of possibility.

There is no more to tell, except that there was great joy on both sides.

We humans could not get over our astonishment that Allie had found the way back to her lodgings on her own. She herself took it for granted, and showed delight, but not a trace of pride.

But then Allie never put on airs.

None of us have seen her since she went to her new home and entered the diplomatic service. But I have heard, through friends who know her present owner, that a rather spoilt little black pen-wiper scurries about in his garden, and that some time ago she became the mother of several more little pen-wipers.

All's well that ends well.

Two Cats in Paris and One in Florence

PUTTYCASS

Puttycass got his name through a slip of the tongue: someone said Puttycass instead of Pussycat. Since then he had never been called anything else, even though, as a Parisian cat, he should really have had a French name.

He was the son of a wild, shy mother cat which frequented the overgrown old garden behind the house we lived in. Once upon a time it had been a large garden, full of tall trees and thick hedges that no one clipped any longer, now divided up as best it could be done between the tenants of the house.

Some of them had a few flowers, where the sun reached them. Others let anything grow as it liked and were satisfied with just a bench. In many places one had to force a path through as if in a jungle.

In the middle of it all lived an old tortoise, a wise animal. In August, when the close Parisian summer was at its hottest, it took up a permanent position under the tap by the wall of the house, where the owners of the gardens came to fetch water. All of them gave the tortoise a shower.

But the cats, who crept about behind the tree-trunks, beneath dark branches heavy with foliage and through thickets of bracken, probably thought they were tigers at the very least.

It was brought to our notice more than once that Puttycass thought he was one.

The mother cat was so wary that nobody was allowed to come near her. She was bad-tempered and dangerous, she spat and scratched. She was not often visible either. Many of the tenants put out food for her, for in Paris people are on the whole very fond of cats. She never touched it until the benefactor was completely out of sight.

She had kittens frequently. When the caretaker found them he killed them so that the property should not turn into a veritable cat farm. But sometimes the mother hid them so well that they would appear only when they were quite large. They would swarm around in the jungle for a while, until they disappeared one by one, left home to look for their own hunting-grounds, and became a part of the enormous city's gigantic wild-cat tribe.

Puttycass was found up in the loft of an old shed. For some reason his mother had abandoned him.

And for some reason the caretaker tempered justice with mercy, perhaps because he looked as if he were going to be handsome.

After some discussion as to who should look after him, he landed with us.

He was still so small that we had to give him milk with a teaspoon, by no means an easy task, as the milk ran in all directions. But not many days passed before Puttycass was drinking from the teaspoon correctly.

The next thing he learned was to go to the toilet in a yellow earthenware dish with sand in it, which became his property. A hard school.

To be lifted by the scruff of the neck, have your nose pushed into the little puddle or pile, be carried rapidly across the room and placed in the dish, to the accompaniment of loud rebukes, was certainly anything but pleasant. Especially when you stood there scratching and clawing the floor as best you could in order to hide the scandal.

To combine the two things, what had to be buried, and the sand that was suitable for doing it, was just the right problem for Puttycass. The solution suited the fastidious, extremely hygienic nature of the cat, so that he caught on quickly. Cats are priggish on this point. Soon we observed Puttycass stepping clumsily about in the dish, doing his duty, a little askew and beyond bounds, but so well intentioned that it could not result in anything but applause. Very soon he was a virtuoso in his dish.

Altogether he evidenced a desire to learn calculated to disarm anybody. He came from the jungle and was originally a completely wild little animal, but no cat could have been more intelligent. I become emotional when I talk about Puttycass, as one does at the memory of gifted individuals who are no longer alive.

The studio we lived in was large, a splendid place for the education of a cat.

Puttycass took his training seriously. From early morning the noise of small paws could be heard going at top speed, galloping all over the studio, high up the walls and down again, back and up the opposite wall, hour after hour.

We continued with our daily pursuits. We went so far in our demands that we insisted on standing at our easel and painting. But when a little cat comes bolting across it all time after time, as if shot from a cannon, knocking it all over as he passes, it is not easy to concentrate.

With the help of some wire netting we divided the studio in two. The idea was that Puttycass could be satisfied with half of it and still have plenty of room. It helped for a short while. But soon, climbing over the netting and obviously finding the arrangement even more fun than before, came Puttycass. Steeplechasing is a select sport.

He grew up into a beautiful young cat, strong and graceful, dignified and mischievous, the pride and joy of the studio.

There is a photograph of him, barely full-grown. He is lying on a basket chair looking straight at you. His fur is white, with a blanket of grey striped with black along his back, his tail, over his ears and a little way down his forehead. Round his eyes the black and grey form an amusing, regular pattern. It looks as if a tiny spectacle arm extends behind each ear. We never talked about his eyes but of his spectacles. If, for instance, he looked at us, his eyes open and bright, he had his big spectacles on; if he narrowed his eyes, he had the small ones.

In the picture he looks out at the world through serious, thoughtful, large spectacles. He looks proud, wise and courageous, and so he was. He was probably afraid of certain things, but then so are the greatest heroes. Heroes see the danger and attack just the same. That's what Puttycass did.

His whiskers and eyebrows are impressive: long and finely attuned. His nose is pink, but that does not show in the photograph, nor that his lovely pads were the same colour.

I know of no finer portrait of a cat than this one.

Every morning he was brushed. To begin with he disliked it, but soon realized it was for his own good as was much else, and lay down of his own accord on the floor when the brush was brought out.

In the end he came to love both the brushing itself, and probably the feeling that resulted from it. A well-treated cat has a great desire to look handsome and groomed. It will gladly accept everything that can contribute to this.

Whether he was capable of concluding that it was due to the brush that he was allowed to lie on any chair he liked, as well as on the divan, I do not know, but it would not surprise me.

Puttycass did not shed hairs at any season of the year. All loose hairs were simply removed.

He possessed two priceless qualities to a high degree: humour and imagination. He soon discovered how tremendously comical we were, when a little cat sprang straight at our legs, not least when we went without stockings in the heat. To fix your teeth and claws in a bare ankle, not so that the blood flowed and there were scratches, but just enough to make the owner of the ankle shriek, jump into the air and look foolish, was an exquisite pleasure.

In all his games he was gentle with us. His claws were

certainly extended now and again, but only out of sheer carelessness. We could see him remembering that this was teasing, not fighting. The claws disappeared, the paws again became velvet paws, *pattes de velour* as we called them.

We talked to Puttycass mainly in French, even though he understood Norwegian and Swedish at an early stage.

For a long time Puttycass knew nothing about the jungle itself, the big garden with many possibilities. You got there through the studio window, and for a long time this was too high. Or you could take the long way round, which demanded maturity and experience. One had to be familiar with a labyrinth. That takes time.

But right outside the door we had a tiny piece of ground, a semicircular flower-bed with a white Japanese anemone, a few petunias, an edging of London pride, and, nearest the house, strong roots of the ivy that had climbed up and covered the whole of the brick wall.

We often sat resting there in the twilight after the chores of the day. Then for Puttycass we turned into heaven knows what mysterious beings, that had to be lain in wait for under the ivy, under the pale shining saucers of the anemone, or under the purple bells of the petunias, so that he could pounce on us in one great bound right over the London pride. Not on the whole of us, naturally. Puttycass was no tiger, after all. But on parts within reach: hands busy in the flower-bed, a bare ankle thoughtlessly swinging up and down.

In fact I remember Puttycass best against a background of flowers and greenery. The summer is long in France. Anyone who owns the smallest patch of garden has plenty of time to spend in it.

I can see Puttycass in the little patch beside the door. I can see him when bigger, creeping between the hedges in the jungle. He positions his forepaws in the way large felines do, the one precisely in front of the other. He has large, staring spectacles which gleam in the twilight and obviously see things of which we are unaware. He makes a tiger-leap and lands on an innocent and incautious moth. Suddenly he climbs up a tree, stretches himself along one of its branches, is really a jungle cat, a tiger, waiting for an unsuspicious prey to come walking along the path beneath.

And I see him sitting between the geraniums in the large window, from where he looks out on the jungle. It became his favourite place when he was indoors. He looked splendid there, as trim and stylish in his bearing as an Egyptian.

We others had to climb on to a chair to water the geraniums. In his best years Puttycass reached the sill in one bound.

At table he sat on a high stool, a painting-stool, so that he was on a level with us and could see what was going on. His paws folded tidily and his tail elegantly coiled around them, he watched attentively, turning his head as the dishes were passed round. From the very beginning he sat irreproachably at table and never begged. If he was passed anything, a piece of brown cheese for instance, which we had caused to be sent from Norway at considerable cost and were miserly with, he would eat it in the delicate manner of a cat, without any mess and without leaving the slightest crumb, lick himself clean and sit as before. Puttycass loved brown cheese.

Of course he was spoilt but, if I may say so, in a tactful and intelligent manner. He never abused his position.

Our meals were a kind of entertainment. He was given his own food in a bowl on the floor and it was cooked in his own private saucepan. In addition to milk he ate mainly liver and lights. For that we preferred not to use our own pans and crockery.

When we came home from shopping, and Puttycass was sitting in his place between the geraniums, his back to the door, he would prick up his ears as soon as he heard us. But he would turn round only when the private saucepan was taken down from the wall. He recognized its clang and considered it a waste of time to move too soon.

When he was fully grown he acquired the habit of going out to fight, as cats will. Then he might stay away for days on end, causing us no little anxiety.

The first time we were quite upset, when he came home

again, thin, his ears in tatters, and with scratches and scars all over him.

There was no mistaking his shame at his condition. He slunk along the wall, making himself small. He had left home an accomplished, well-groomed young cat. Now he looked as if he had been lying in the gutter.

He would eat a little, lie down and sleep for a long time. He ate and slept again, did nothing else for several days and made himself small and invisible as best he could. Until suddenly one day he stretched himself, sat up on the window-sill in one bound and pretended that nothing was the matter.

'Aha,' said old Madame Rousseau, who was our nearest neighbour and loved Puttycass as much as we did. 'We come home and let ourselves be looked after. Until the next time.'

And, quite right, at certain intervals the desire to fight would come over him again. He would vanish. When he appeared once more, he was in a more or less distressing state. It was a side of his nature that we had to accept.

Each time we received him as one receives a prodigal son, with good food and without referring to what had happened.

We could see that he was thrashed repeatedly. But we never doubted that he gave as good as he got. He was certainly not the only one to come home with his ears in tatters. He was far from being a coward.

Or was he afraid of Pyramus, the big dog a little farther down the street? Pyramus was so much larger than Puttycass, and a dog into the bargain. There are limits to what one will tackle. Personally I believe Puttycass felt disgust rather than fear.

When Pyramus arrived, he would hurry so quickly up the stairs to the loft where we had our beds that we didn't actually see him go. He was just up there all of a sudden.

There he stood on the highest step, on tall legs, arching his back, his fur standing on end like a feather duster, while he kept his eye on the studio.

Down below unprecedented things were happening. Pyramus was walking around in an offhand manner, sniffing at everything, eating, merely in passing, with a single curl of the tongue, all the food from Puttycass's dish: the meal he himself should have eaten in a finicking manner, in tiny pieces, critically searching for the tastiest and best of them.

Pyramus did not so much as see Puttycass. He was the epitome of the bully who, thanks to his size and his strength, assumes that he can take whatever liberties he pleases.

When he had finished sniffing about and taking what there was to take, he went on his way, untouched by the feelings of others. At the corner of the house he lifted his hind leg.

On one single occasion I remember Puttycass being afraid of a person: a completely ordinary and innocent man who came with a parcel.

What was fearsome or unsavoury about him was never discovered. We observed nothing. On the contrary, we liked him. But at the very sight of him Puttycass instantly bolted up the stairs to the loft, standing up there, fur on end, arching his back until the terrible individual had gone.

Perhaps it was his voice. Perhaps Puttycass's imagination was playing tricks on him as it often did and he thought he saw something that didn't exist.

That he did not like strangers unreservedly was another matter. Like most animals he was jealous, and did not like us to be too taken up with others.

He could do one trick, the kind that has to be learnt. It was not complicated. It would be wrong to say it demanded great intelligence. But since he was a cat it cost him effort. Cats are independent and lovers of freedom as no other animals are. Cleanliness and good manners accord with their nature and they learn them willingly. But otherwise they brook no interference and act exactly as they please. Who ever heard of circus cats?

When Puttycass agreed to run after a cork we threw, and carried it back to us time after time, it must have been because he thought it was fun, and condescended to do it for that reason. Such fun that he often found the cork himself and laid it in front of us, as a sign that now we could surely play for a while?

We threw it. He rushed off and came trotting back with the

cork in his mouth, self-important and dignified beyond all bounds.

I do not really understand how we could have had the heart to leave Puttycass. One should not leave animals for long. In that case an easy, quick death is best for them.

Our excuse was that we intended to return in a year's time, that we did not know what was going to happen to France, and that we left Puttycass in good hands.

In the autumn of 1913 we moved to Italy. He was boarded out with Monsieur and Madame Rousseau, who were our next-door neighbours. He was used to going in and out of their apartment at will.

For a long time all went well. We received little letters about how Puttycass was. We sent little letters back, with money for his keep, for the Rousseaus were poor people living on a tiny pension.

While we were away the war broke out, the war we, in our naïveté, called the Great War. We could not imagine a greater war, a worse war. Not at that time.

Puttycass became a war casualty. At any rate there is reason to believe so.

Shortly before we were to travel home we received a distressing letter. He had disappeared, not out on a fighting spree; he had completely vanished. All searching, all questioning in the neighbourhood had been in vain. All sitting up at night too, in case he should come home then. Nobody had reacted to the notice the Rousseaus had put up outside the house.

We do not know what became of him. But when there is war, life becomes more dangerous, existence more uncertain for a cat too. It is a reasonable guess that Puttycass, large and handsome in his beautiful coat, had been a temptation to someone. Gradually more and more people became short of money and food. A cat's skin is always worth a few francs. That's what we imagined had happened.

It was sad to come from Italy in springtime, where there was as yet no war, to winter-grey, blacked-out Paris. Life and the people there had altered since we last lived there, a great gravity prevailed, and we could hear the thunder of distant guns.

It was the Battle of Soissons. It was February 1915.

It was sad in the empty, cold studio, with no young, beautiful cat, purring and friendly, to meet us.

Sometimes I still miss Puttycass.

THE NIGHT PROWLER

What were we to call it if not the Night Prowler, *Le Noctambule*? The name came automatically. No other name would do.

We never saw it during the day. But a short while after sunset, when twilight fell, when the air above the large garden was so full of scent that the heavy atmosphere of the city had to give way for a few hours, and one could believe, with a little imagination, that one was in the country, then the Night Prowler arrived.

It stalked along slowly, a huge old tabby cat, it also a tiger in the jungle, reserved and wary, unapproachable.

It came to, or almost to, our door. It could curl up under the ivy or in the flower-bed, and stay there undisturbed, even though we walked past quite close. But if we stretched out a hand to stroke it, it immediately got to its feet and left, without haste, but firmly dismissive. If we attempted to put out something for it to eat, it never touched it while we were watching. The food had usually gone by the morning, but we never knew whether it or other cats had taken it.

Unfriendly as it was, we had the impression that basically it trusted us. Later on this proved to be correct. It simply did not want the kind of friendship that can easily become intrusive. Both this cat and Puttycass's mother must have had bitter experience where humans were concerned. They were not to be allowed to come too close.

Madame Rousseau was of the opinion that Puttycass was

the Night Prowler's son, an assertion which it was of course impossible to verify. In the first place it was no use asking. In the second, cats quickly forget their own family relationships, as far as one can judge.

One thing is certain: both of them were characters.

We came to know the Night Prowler only when it fell ill.

It had not turned up for a long time. But suddenly one evening it miaowed outside our door. Puttycass was sleeping the sleep of the just on a painting-stool, so it could not have been him.

We were more than astonished when we opened the door and saw who it was.

The Night Prowler, the shy cat who would never allow itself to be touched by anybody, was standing there asking us for help. It miaowed, it looked at us.

It was already quite dark, but we could see that something was seriously wrong. It was nothing but skin and bone, and had caught some kind of skin disease, so that patches of hair had fallen off. It looked ugly and pathetic.

We dared not touch it. Not immediately. Such things are unpleasant to deal with, and may be infectious and dangerous. But we were very upset to see the Night Prowler in this condition. We felt flattered as well, because it had come to us in its need. After all, it didn't have dealings with just anybody.

That evening we had to leave it without help, there was no alternative. We hoped it would not give us up, but come again the next day.

In Paris, in an emergency, one goes first to the chemist to ask for advice. There they are always interested and helpful, whether it concerns man or beast. They assist you as far as they can. We described the Night Prowler's condition and were given, in addition to firm orders not to touch it with our bare hands, a yellow ointment, a wooden spatula, and a bottle with some kind of cleansing solution.

The evening came, and we stood there armed, wearing old gloves. We waited nervously.

We became even more nervous when we caught sight of it

approaching, slow and dignified as ever. Now we would see whether it still counted on us, or whether it thought we were a couple of ninnies it was no good appealing to. Animals must often have that opinion of us.

But the Night Prowler had not given us up. The Night Prowler stopped and miaowed. The Night Prowler submitted to having yellow ointment pasted all over it. The ointment must have had an immediately healing effect, for the timid cat stood completely still; it even twisted and turned and lifted its paws so that we should reach all the sore places.

When the treatment was over, we put out a saucer of milk. The Night Prowler drank the milk, licked its lips and went its way.

We felt more than flattered. We felt honoured.

The next evening was decisive. Then the Night Prowler had to be washed before we could put more ointment on. It was supposed to be done without handling it, and cats hate getting wet. The task was not exactly easy.

We wound a cloth round the spatula and stood ready.

The Night Prowler arrived. The Night Prowler submitted to being washed too, even though we did it clumsily and with little expertise. The Night Prowler was covered in ointment, drank some milk, and even accepted a little food.

We, on our part, began to feel self-important.

Evening after evening it came to our door. If the door was closed, it miaowed. The Night Prowler was desperate. Either it had to let itself be helped or go under.

It is not easy for a proud and independent nature to seek help from others. It has to make an effort, its need has to be great, and all other alternatives closed. It is a position of trust, an honour to give assistance, but it is seldom understood that way.

We imagined that we understood. In fact we were no better than most benefactors. Even as we were puffed up with self-importance because the cat was improving, getting a fine coat again and putting on weight, we were doing it a great injustice in our minds.

Supposing it decided to move in with us. Cats are peculiar that way. If they find people or a house they like, it is scarcely possible to get them to abandon the idea.

We could not have two cats, especially since Puttycass had been raising his hackles out of jealousy every time the Night Prowler came, and had to be kept under lock and key while we tended it.

We were afraid we would never be rid of it again: the usual anxiety of the affluent when they lend a hand to their indigent brothers.

We need not have been anxious. From the day the Night Prowler recovered completely it walked past our door once again, looking neither to right nor left. It might sit in the flower-bed for a while, as before. But it would not take food, not while we were watching, and it would not allow itself to be stroked. The fact that it had eaten in our presence was more a form of politeness on its part, a form of appreciation, and something it was forced to do if it were to survive. A sick cat is unable to go hunting.

It was no sponger. When it was well again it withdrew. I think it liked us. I think it had lived with people once upon a time, and would have liked to do so again. But it was too sensitive to intrude. And too wise.

There is an old proverb that says, Today's guest is tomorrow's pest. Naturally the Night Prowler did not know of it. But it must have had an experience that amounted to the same thing.

Only those who possess true pride are capable of suspecting it in others. It was to our shame that we had doubted it in the Night Prowler.

THE CAT IN FLORENCE

The cat in Florence was never given a proper name. We simply called him Kitty. That's Swedish and corresponds to the Norwegian 'Puss'.

He was the most miserable of all the wild cats that passed

through the garden where we lived. Italian cities are full – or were full at that time – of wild cats.

The garden was old and very fine, with a pool in the middle and many kinds of beautiful Mediterranean trees such as pine and palm, and large flowering bushes of camellia and rhododendron. A rich American owned it and the house but was seldom there, and he rented it out for long periods at a time.

An Italian by the name of Armando was employed to look after it.

Armando was not kind to the wild cats. As soon as he caught sight of one he would throw stones at it. His aim was good, too. He hit them. We felt most sorry for the one that later on became our Kitty. He was scraggier, more scared, more pathetic than any of the others.

We could not help putting out food for him; that is to say, we tried to feed him. A long time elapsed before he dared approach it. From a safe place beneath the bushes he sat and stared at the spread with hungry yellow eyes. When one day he finally dared to come out for a morsel, he crept back quickly, as if with his prey. This cat was extremely afraid of humans, which after all was not surprising. But we had won a small victory.

The final victory was won with French sardines; or rather, with the remains of them, skin, bones and oil. We ate the sardines ourselves. There are limits to what cats should be treated to. But we remembered how eager Puttycass always became when he saw us opening a tin of sardines.

Whether the sight or the smell awoke dim memories in Kitty of better days, I do not know. The fact is that on that day his resistance was broken down. He licked the tin thoroughly clean, licked his lips thoroughly, and sat waiting for more. It had been *too* good.

From then on we were able to approach him. Not long after, he would come running as soon as he saw us with his food. He hid under the bushes all the time, watching to see when we would come out.

One fine day he followed us in, tentatively, cautiously, lifting one paw at a time, as cats do in unknown territory. The inspection turned out to our advantage, he became our cat, and took the place of Puttycass whom we had left behind.

With that, Armando's persecution ceased, and Kitty had an easy time of it. Soon he became a magnificent-looking cat, his fur thick and in shining condition. When cats are given sufficient food they produce plenty of saliva, so that they can lick themselves handsome.

Kitty was not so quick to learn as Puttycass, not distinguished and reserved like the Night Prowler. He lacked tact and good manners, soon started whining and demanding, and acquired cheeky habits. When we came home from Porta Romana with our purchases Kitty would meet us at the gate, yowling, miaowing and jumping after the package of liver or lights so violently that we could hardly manage to get any farther.

No, it was quite different from when Puttycass used to sit between the geraniums in his window, moving his ears very slightly, never his head, until he heard the clang of his own saucepan among the others. But Puttycass had had an easy life almost from the start. He had not slunk around, hungry and persecuted, had never been deeply humiliated by poverty and ill-treatment. For him well-being was natural and inevitable.

Kitty never learnt to believe in his carefree situation, or to understand that if he could be patient for only a moment, until the paper was unwrapped and the food prepared, he would probably be satisifed.

He had a tendency to theft, too, to which Puttycass never stooped. That again was connected with Kitty's former wretchedness; he was used to taking whatever he chanced to find.

Then there was the blue quilt: a down quilt brought from home in North Norway. He was strictly forbidden to lie on it. Kitty had a basket and various chairs besides. He was brushed every morning, did not shed loose hair, and could lie wherever he wished. Except on the beds, except on the blue quilt.

But Kitty adored the quilt. Of all good things to lie on or under, the quilt was the favourite. Time after time Kitty was caught there, and chased down again with increasing severity. One day he was given a proper slap. The limit had been set, and that was the end of it.

After that Kitty kept within bounds for a while, as far as we could see, that is. But . . . one afternoon we heard steady, slightly distant purring. To begin with we could not understand where it was coming from; Kitty was nowhere to be seen.

At first we couldn't believe our ears, but finally we had to admit it. The purring came from under the quilt.

Kitty had decided to go the back way, as one might say, and had quietly crept under the bed and jumped up from the side against the wall.

Nobody would have chased him away, not at that point, at any rate, if Kitty, lying there warm and soft and comfortable, had not gradually felt blissful beyond all bounds, so that he was unable to hide it any longer. He purred so that he positively roared.

We had to laugh. It is always amusing when animals reveal their thoughts; amusing, too, when anyone, animal or human, is not as cunning as he thinks himself to be.

Kitty had no idea that we had heard him, and the expression on his face when the quilt was mercilessly pulled away was priceless. He slunk down before he was slapped, slunk out and stayed out for a long time.

He never attempted it again.

He was a touching cat in many ways. The only people he trusted were ourselves. No one else was allowed to pick him up; he did not voluntarily jump up and lie down in anyone else's lap. And what is more, when we left home, Kitty always accompanied us for part of the way like a dog, up to where the proper streets of the city began, for we lived in a suburb. He would creep under some bushes, always at the same spot, and lie there watching us go.

Often hours might pass before we returned. Kitty would be sitting there still, would come out from his hiding-place purring loudly, and rub up against our legs, happy to have us home again.

What he was thinking during all those hours under the bushes, it is impossible to tell, but they must have been anxious thoughts. He had remembered the whole time that we were away; perhaps he also remembered dimly how miserable he had been before we arrived.

In certain respects he was far more patient than might be expected of a young cat. For he was young. We realized this after he had been eating proper food for a while and had turned into a magnificent-looking animal. Then he became playful and lively and disappeared on fighting expeditions. A cat's a cat, after all.

Old cats are often patient, for they are wise, and have the self-control of the wise in all situations. Young cats can seldom count patience among their virtues.

Kitty could, as long as food was not involved. Perhaps adversity had taught him that one gets nothing for nothing, that life is not just a game but demands effort for what it gives.

At any rate, the fact is that he posed for us. He would sit still obediently for long periods at a time. Of course his patience broke down occasionally, but with a little persuasion, a little petting, he would do it again.

The result was a sculpture, which is now in the National Museum in Stockholm. Kitty has gone down to posterity, albeit anonymously. The sculpture is called simply *Cat.*

The day arrived when we had to leave Florence to travel back to Paris. The war was on, the message that Puttycass had disappeared had reached us. With heavy hearts we were forced to take the decision to destroy Kitty. We had no one to hand him on to. We did not want him to be homeless, persecuted and wretched again after his carefree life with us. We had been given a lesson in what can happen to animals in times of uncertainty.

Kitty was put in a basket. Nobody other than ourselves would have been able to persuade him into the basket and get him to sit there with the lid on. It made it even more hurtful that we could lure him out on his last journey. But we had no choice. To leave him behind alone would have been indefensible. That would have been even worse.

It was the master of the house who took him away. I was excused. But I know he was given a quick, easy death. The vet gave him an injection. He took a few steps and fell over lifeless on to his side, without a sound.

He left an emptiness behind him, as happens when trusting creatures have shown us confidence, affection and gratitude.

The Broad versus the Narrow Outlook

'They're torturing Leif in the cellar, Mother.'

Astrid rushes in, upset and out of breath. 'They've taken him down to Uncle Torbjørn's cellar and they're torturing him.'

'Who's taken him down to the cellar?'

'Erling and Odd, of course. Fritz Heiler's there, making them do it. Hermann and Little Rudolf and Karl are helping to hold him. Hermine and Lise are watching.'

'Torturing him? I suppose they're fighting again?'

'They've tied his hands together and stuck a stick in between and they're twisting it round. Isn't that torture? You *must* come, Mother, he's white as a sheet.'

Mrs Olavsen has straightened up from her squatting position by the flower-bed she was sowing, brushes earth from her fingers and hurries up through the garden, tired and angry. This is the last straw if it's true. This too.

He will not admit that the Heilers are behind everything here. But none of us will admit it. Because it isn't the Heilers really. . . .

Mrs Olavsen hurries for dear life, the mother in her gathering itself together, ready to fight. Up through the garden, along the neglected part, which is not hers and which she hates, round the corner of the house. She bends down in front of the cellar window, Astrid pointing.

Down in the semi-darkness she can glimpse Leif's face, withdrawn, defiant, white, clenched over the pain; Fritz Heiler's with twitching mouth, a glitter in his eyes that makes her see red; the others' pleasurably excited. They are crowded round Leif, gripping him tight. Mrs Olavsen almost drives her hand through the glass, but comes to her senses and bangs on it with her knuckles. They all look up.

Shortly afterwards they come out: Fritz first, his hands in his trouser pockets and with a slack, dissipated look on his face, Leif with the same pale defiance, the others still excited. Fritz sweeps his cap off his head and is about to walk past.

'What's going on here?'

'Going on? We're playing.'

'What sort of game?'

'We – we're testing each other to see how much we can stand.' Fritz sneers derisively.

'All of you against one, and big against small. How very brave! Get along with you, Fritz, you've no business here, nor have the rest of you. You can play that kind of game at home. Come along, children.' Mrs Olavsen turns and goes, followed by Astrid and Leif, the latter stony-faced. She hears Fritz's laughter, and someone else calling out 'tattlebottom' and 'sissy'. And when she reaches the corner of the house a cocky 'We're allowed to be here because of Uncle Torbjørn and Uncle Rudolf, so there.'

She does not say a word. Neither do the children. But when they have reached the safety of the veranda steps Leif says, 'You shouldn't have interfered, Mother. I can manage. Don't phone Aunt Augusta, Mother.'

'I can't let it go on, Leif. It's turned into sheer persecution. Let me see your wrists. They're swelling up. The other day you came home with a bleeding nose and mouth. The time before . . .'

'It'll only get worse if you phone. Just so's you know. And I *shall* hold out. It's important that I hold out. They can't *kill* me.'

Leif didn't cry in the cellar. Now he is not far from doing so. The clenched little boy's mouth is quivering. Impulsively his mother cups his face in her hands.

'It will not get worse, I promise. Go down to the jetty, both of you, and see what Tom and Guri are doing.' Mrs Olavsen sits down, drained with emotion. Above her she can hear women's voices in uninterrupted conversation, then all of a sudden boys' voices.

'Mother!'

'*Yes*, Leif.'

The children leave. Immediately afterwards the telephone rings. Trembling, Mrs Olavsen picks up the receiver. From it comes the voice of her sister-in-law, Mrs Vefring, earnest and protective. 'There's been another scene, I hear. My boys came to me themselves to tell me. You see, that's how they are, honest and truthful. If only you and your family would see things as they are, adapt yourselves a little, everything would work out, Marie. I must tell you that Leif had offended the others' sense of justice. Growing children *are* hurt by things like that. But imagine taking that sort of thing seriously, boys will be boys. Leif needs to be toughened a bit. As for forbidding the Heiler children to come here, after all we live here too, you know.'

Without a word Mrs Olavsen replaces the receiver. She has harboured many kinds of feelings for the Vefrings over the years, has laughed at them, felt sorry for them, been a little afraid of them, now she hates them.

She goes to the veranda door and looks out. Early spring, the air full of the scents of new growth and of smoke from burning off the old grass. Below her lies the garden, laid out round several huge stones rooted in the earth. The knuckles of the land, her husband often remarks, slapping them affectionately, as one slaps a horse. One of them has a large flat surface facing south. Espaliered plums, the finest for miles around, his pride and joy, ripen there in early autumn.

Between the stones are fruit trees and currant bushes, some birch and lilac, which are just coming into leaf. Where larger surfaces lie open to the sun there are beds for plants, and elsewhere a lawn with a paved path leading to it and room for a table and benches. At the bottom of the garden the shore with large stones and smooth rock, jetty, boat and boat-house, and the fjord, shining like a mirror. Mrs Olavsen can hear the children on the jetty.

In all modesty a lovely garden, if only the Vefrings would

keep their part of it tidy. Not a spadeful of earth has been turned by them yet this year. The fruit trees are standing in the rank, uncut turf, beards growing on their trunks from neglect. Last year's tall brown weeds and withered leaves are rampant everywhere. It doesn't take long for a garden to turn into an untidy wilderness.

If only she could do something about it with wire brush and spray, prune and dig. Get the old trees to produce what they can again. Not have to watch the decline any longer.

But her husband likes to say 'My word, we've got a lot out of this poor soil between these rocks. It's cost us hard work, it's cost us a few loads of manure and earth, but name a place where you'd rather live.'

He usually says it when he's leaning on his spade for a moment, or on the fork, or the rake, relaxing and looking about him, wearing his old suit which is stiff with manure and green with scum.

And Mrs Olavsen knows of no other place where she'd rather live. In spite of the Vefrings, she doesn't know of one. A good place for the children to grow up in. A good place for them to come back to some day, when they have flown from the nest, to come home to again at intervals, maybe bringing new little children who will call her Granny. Good to grow old in, when that time comes. It's often been a struggle. She remembers the years without water, without help in the house, without an electric cooking stove; she remembers the winters before they had central heating. But the improvements were made, one after another. Time and again the greyness of everyday was broken by fresh happiness, by a new improvement that made life easier for them all. And nowhere do you get the same view of the fjord as you do here.

She goes down the veranda steps, turns, and looks up at the house. No urban villa, but an old-fashioned ship's captain's house. Behind it tower the enormous crowns of ancient trees, behind them the blue ridge of the hills.

An old idea occurs to her, mechanically, out of habit: buy out the Vefrings, redecorate the upper storey. Leif will be fourteen in the autumn. He must have his own room soon, Astrid did at that age. They could take it piecemeal and gradually. Tom and Guri will grow up one day too. Maybe the large, sunny room with the balcony would be right for the unknown little children whom Mrs Olavsen vaguely imagines running in and out in eight or ten years' time. A new bathroom could be put in next door to it. If only her husband could get that promotion soon. If only the debt for the last repair were paid off. If only she had got so far as to have a regular profit on the currant bushes. She needs new strawberry plants, new raspberry canes. Better order them from Eriksen's nursery tomorrow.

Everything is suddenly swept away by a terrible vision: the earthbound stones dynamited away, the old-fashioned house robbed of its sun, squashed in between tall, urban buildings, traffic, crowds of people, dust and noise. She hears piercing steamer sirens and Augusta Vefring's protective voice, remembers Fritz Heiler saying 'We're allowed to because of Uncle Torbjørn and Uncle Rudolf, so there', she recalls the expression on Leif's face when they were torturing him.

She puts her hand to her breast, her heart is hammering painfully. Vefrings cannot be bought out any more. It's too late. They have allied themselves with the power of money.

'It's no use blocking progress, Halvard,' says Vefring, the solicitor. He fixes Olavsen with his unemotional little eyes, which Olavsen thinks resemble those of a pig, and rocks to and fro on his heels.

'Don't bring in progress again. That's not what we were talking about.'

'Yes, that *is* what we were talking about. The quarrel between the boys is only another side of the same problem. The moment you and your family give in to – well, shall we say, the demands of the times – it'll vanish. The young are always the same. They go in for everything heart and soul. I repeat, you'll never get an offer like this a second time. You know very well there's more than one person after land here, Smith on the island, Hoff at Røyseland. You can't expect anything else with the site we have. None of them will offer as much as Rudolf Heiler, if I judge them correctly. You have the chance of doing a fine piece of business, of making money, to put it bluntly. You'll be almost a free man on your land. The house will remain standing, the garden won't be touched, not much at least, Heiler must have tenants, there's a place left open for you on the board. Smith and Hoff . . .'

'Stop that nonsense about Smith and Hoff. Neither Smith nor Hoff have anything to do with this, and the place on the board can go to the devil. I'll never sell the family property. God knows, we've talked about it more than enough. Go upstairs and give your boys a spanking, go down into your garden and dig up the worst of it, and you'll be doing something useful. Good evening, Torbjørn.'

'Wait a moment, now, Halvard. With these changes, with the development of the plots that Heiler's planning, the whole place will start booming. There are a good many of us who can see that. In a place like this there shouldn't be a little bit of gardening, a little fishing on the side from a boat in the evenings. There should be something profitable, a bathing resort, hotels. Don't you understand that you have to think big, man?'

'No, I don't. This place will boom without that kind of development. It's been booming as long as I can remember, it grows naturally at its own pace. Development? That's just what you want to prevent, you and Heiler and the others that the two of you have talked round. We have good roads, water, electric light, the telephone, not far to go to the school or the doctor or the shops. It was different when you and I were boys. It would be a shame to touch this place.'

'Well, well, well,' says Vefring, changing the subject and suddenly staring into the distance as if seeing visions. 'Things are different on Smith's island, let me tell you. They've had a quay for the steamers for a long time. Everything's rising in value, people over there are getting rich. With our possibilities we could go way beyond them, dominate the whole fjord. But here we are, stagnating in a backwater.'

'Here we are, living comfortably in peace and quiet. Our children will grow up healthy and strong here. We have buses, boats, what do we want with a quay for steamers? If you and Rudolf can't live without one, for God's sake build one on his own beach.'

'Too out-of-the-way. Too shallow as well, would be too expensive. We must have a stopping-place sooner or later, if we're to outstrip Smith and Hoff. And here you sit, blocking the whole thing. Is that having a social conscience? Is that keeping up with the times? When we have a man like Rudolf Heiler among us – imagination, a broad outlook, courage to take responsibility . . .'

'Yes, worse luck! A ruthless climber, a crazy fellow. I wish we could be rid of the whole Heiler gang. You've got mixed up in some funny things in your time, Torbjørn, but I'd never have believed you'd get mixed up with that lot. Who, for God's sake, says we've got to outstrip Smith and Hoff? What sort of nonsense is that?'

Vefring isn't touchy, he doesn't take offence. He comes a little closer and remarks confidentially, 'I don't suppose, Halvard, that you happen to have an understanding with Smith already? It's been hinted at.'

'Are you out of your mind, man? You and Heiler are hinting at it, nobody else. That's the sort of thing you believe people are likely to do.'

'It looks like it. Just take Andersson who owns the land to the east of you.'

'Yes, at his age . . .'

'He's not too old to understand the idea of progress behind it. For the time being he's promised us free right of way with all kinds of materials . . .'

'In that case he'll have his children to reckon with.'

'Not all of them. Besides, it's the old man who decides things in that household. They have respect for their father over there.'

'And you're saying that he believes this rumour of an agreement between Smith and me? Is he in his dotage already? Besides, I thought he had Hoff of Røyseland on the brain?'

'Andersson wants to keep every avenue open.'

'And gets mixed up in this business with you and Rudolf. The right thing to do, I suppose? Do go home and start digging your garden, Torbjørn. It looks so dreadfully neglected.'

'Be a waste of time with all these changes going on. I don't mind admitting that neither Augusta nor I has ever been interested in gardening.'

'What does interest you? What kind of people do you do business for? Fortune hunters, unscrupulous characters . . .'

'Are you referring to Rudolf?'

'I am referring to Rudolf. You could at least go home and feel ashamed of yourself and try to do some honest work again, instead of acting as an errand-boy for the Heilers. You'll find you're not playing the part you expect. Anyway, what will that damned Rudolf pay you for your soul? We can work out roughly what he's offering for the land. Then I'd like to remind you of something. When I painted the house a few years ago, I painted the whole house. When I installed central heating, you got it too. I haven't expected any compensation, but I didn't expect you to attack me from behind either. The house was built by our grandfather. In my part downstairs it's still comfortable. I've kept up with the times in my own way. In your part upstairs it's dilapidated and not very pleasant. Augusta and I inherited the place. You're not only her husband, you're our cousin . . .'

'Augusta shares my view of things.'

'Yes, well, she's never been particularly bright, I'm afraid. But this stupidity is evidently catching. Good evening.'

Olavsen departs. He is wearing his ugly old suit and is carrying a rake in his hand. The evening light, cool and green, shines on him through the ancient tree-tops in the garden. At first Vefring looks innocent, then a dangerous look comes into his eyes and he calls, 'Heiler sends his greetings. To you and Marie.'

'Thank you very much.' Olavsen disappears round the corner of the house. Vefring remains standing for a while, muttering between his teeth. It sounds something like idiot, reactionary, just you wait, you fool, world's got no use for people like you, you'll soon find out.

He does an about turn, and fairly marches up the steps, red in the face.

'Well?' asks Mrs Olavsen anxiously, raking leaves for the little bonfire Olavsen had lit. Crackling, it sends a delicate little plume of smoke straight up in the air, and is obviously as pleasing to God as Abel's sacrifice was in his day. And it smells of spring like nothing else.

'Impudent as the devil. Brought greetings from Rudolf, if you please. To you in particular.'

'Well, we can't send greetings to Rudolf's wife in particular.'

'Good lord, you can't criticize the man for that.'

'Yes, Halvard, you can criticize the man for that. At his age respectable, normal men have wives and children. And they don't get this megalomania, they have other things to think about. Since he came into the business it's been flourishing as never before, they say. Why isn't that enough for him? Isn't it possible to earn money without using it to destroy others?'

'He's not going to destroy us.'

'Soon he *will* have destroyed us. It's impossible to live here any more. They'll kill our children,' says Marie, possessed by the terrible far-sightedness of women.

'We shall have to fight.'

'Haven't we fought enough for all this and against the Vefrings and their foolishness? Do we have to fight for our crystal-clear rights as well?'

'Looks like it. We shan't be alone. People are up in arms all over the place, many of them are relying on us now. This is where they want the quay to be built, this is the centre of their strategy. Chin up, Marie! As long as we refuse, Augusta and Torbjørn won't get anywhere. As for the children, you see how the children are taking it. They're already fighting tooth and nail.'

The central area of the old enclosures belongs to the Heiler family. It is a large, uneven plot, where sons and daughters, gradually growing up and marrying, have built their own houses but still managed to live in the style of the wealthy, each on his little rise. In the middle stands the gloomy house in the Gothic style of the 1870s. Old William Heiler built it for himself when he got so rich selling majolica jugs, brass shields, knick-knacks and bric-à-brac that he was able to start calling himself a wholesaler. It has pinnacles and towers, projections, leaded panes, and a loopholed parapet. Above the main door a double-headed eagle in relief.

Nobody really had anything against the Heilers until they began to take over other people's land. They were disliked for it, and got a reputation for being grasping, conceited and inconsiderate, and certainly not discriminating in their choice of means. They nibbled their way outwards, a piece here, a piece there. The Heilers never sold. People who had never imagined such a thing happening, found themselves their neighbours. Nobody doubts any longer that there is planning behind it, persevering, consistent planning. And where old Heiler used to take one step at a time, Rudolf takes a leap.

He is the kind of person who knows how to surround himself with mystery. You scarcely ever see him, only his car, a long, dark blue seven-seater gliding quickly and soundlessly past. Nevertheless, few appearances are so sharply imprinted in the general consciousness as his: a nose projecting at right angles from his face, narrow, piercing eyes, a forelock and a small moustache. In addition a kind of landed proprietor's uniform, a windcheater with flaps and straps high and low, jackboots and peaked cap.

He is engaged in big deals, throws money around, and according to rumour, earns it. The family has several adult sons in the firm and on its land. They take orders from Rudolf, the relative whom they welcomed among them some years ago. Understand it if you can. It must be something like what used to be called sorcery in the olden days.

They say that the whole concern was on a weak footing until he took over the management; that the sons were pulling in different directions, that disintegration threatened. It was a blessing that Rudolf had been able to unite them all, say those who see it that way.

It's curious, in any case, that the mysterious, powerful, almost invisible Rudolf should be identical with the poorly dressed schoolboy who was visiting at the time of the embarrassing story about the Valeurs' kitchen garden. The Heilers wanted to take it over and turn it into a tennis-court for their flock of young people. Valeur said no. He had worked hard in it, got it going satisfactorily and the last thing he was thinking of was selling. One afternoon the Heiler boys, Rudolf in their midst, stormed the kitchen garden and managed to trample down large areas of it. There was widespread indignation, although even at that time there were those who thought that the Heilers were, in a way, within their rights. The quarrel over who was really at fault continued endlessly, and the compensation for the damage was sheer comedy. The Heilers managed to wriggle out of most of it by making the excuse of difficulties just at that time. Wealthy people like that!

'"Wish me strength to complete my task, madam" is what he answers when I say what a superhuman task it is to fight against sheer ignorance. "Wish me strength".'

Augusta Vefring is holding forth in the middle of Mrs Olavsen's drawing-room and has not been invited to sit down.

She has pale blue eyes, which she opens wide when she speaks, and curls, dyed light yellow. They contrast sadly with her face, which is simultaneously childish and prematurely old. Her clothes are somewhat fanciful and her voice easily takes on a tone of pathos. 'That silly woman,' says Olafsen of his sister when he is really irritated with her.

Otherwise her errand is that there has been trouble again, unfortunately. Yesterday Leif was hit on the forehead by a stone, nobody is denying that. The day before yesterday he was rolled in the clay ditch, nobody is denying that either. Astrid has been bullied on her way to and from school, pushed and pulled and shot at with peas. But everything has its psychological background, children will be children. Leif will not stop behaving arrogantly and offensively, he will not accept facts. If only the children could be a little reasonable. Transition? Of course, but we're all subject to the laws of transition, as Ibsen says.

'Transformation,' Mrs Olavsen corrects her drily.

'Now then, we're not going to quibble over words, Marie. Wouldn't it be better to take each other by the hand? To face the future confidently together? To build up, not pull in different directions? Look what a positive contribution can lead to! Heiler came here yesterday and suggested redecorating the whole flat upstairs, new wallpaper everywhere, modernizing the kitchen and bathroom, everything that we've never been able to afford.'

Will the Vefrings be allowed to choose colours and wallpapers? Yes, well, that is to say, in these circumstances one will have to take Rudolf's taste into consideration. He has a weakness for the grandiose, the pretentious. But Mrs Vefring does too, to be honest. How was it, weren't the Olavsens thinking about alterations too, even rebuilding? Because in that case it would definitely be best to co-operate, wouldn't it? Not at the moment? Oh, well. . . .

So far Marie has just coldly inserted an occasional question. Now she remarks, 'I'm sure pretentious wallpaper in rooms with low, slanting ceilings will look attractive.'

Mrs Vefring has to laugh at that. The greatness in Heiler's ideas is precisely the preservation of the old within the framework of the new. Those are the sorts of principles *he* follows. No, Smith is the one who has misused his power. And what about Hoff, no better than a barbarian! What did you say? No comparison with Heiler? Marie, Marie, don't you understand, he's saving us from those two? With our situation we can't expect to be sufficient unto ourselves for ever. Sooner or later we shall *have* to become part of a larger unit. It will happen in a satisfactory, happy manner. The old house will be left standing, the whole area will start prospering in a way we can all share.'

'Smith is well liked.' Marie forces herself to speak calmly. 'He gets on well with his neighbours. The Smiths have traditions, they use their wealth with good sense. But this upstart of yours, this Rudolf, ought to limit himself to earning money with his bric-à-brac. If he starts making big gestures, he'll only bring disaster.'

Mrs Vefring is flushing angrily, a patch of red on each cheek. 'The Heilers' traditions are just as old as certain others, if not older,' she asserts, sticking out her bosom on their behalf. 'It's high time they were given a position here that matches those traditions. You ought to express yourself a little more carefully, Marie my dear. It may not be quite so pleasant one day to have been the person who only opposed everything. Upstart, did you say? The Heilers are high-minded people, but they do not suffer fools gladly.'

That was a threat, thinks Mrs Olavsen. She says, 'I'm aware they show no consideration. Traditions? Such people have no traditions. Well, traditions of piracy, perhaps. Goodbye, Augusta.'

'Goodbye, Marie.' And Mrs Vefring leaves. At the door she turns. 'I wanted to give you a hint. As your sister-in-law. Besides, you could have got that extension built now, the one you've been dreaming about for so many years. I'm only mentioning it.'

There are many ways. . . .

Workers have moved in upstairs. They are hammering, knocking, dragging ladders around, putting buckets down hard on the floor. In all this clatter Vefring tramps about, the jackboots he affects easily recognizable.

Out of doors a sudden, warm summer is in full spate. There has not been such a flowering for many years; the air is full of scent and the murmur of bees, the nights are light. It is nearly midsummer, the season one looks forward to all the rest of the year.

In the Vefrings' part of the garden myriads of dandelions have gone to seed. When the wind is in a certain direction, the down from them whirls in clouds across to the Olavsens'. It's easy to see that the fight to the death, which Olavsen has carried on for many years against just this kind of weed, will prove to have been in vain by next summer.

One day digging starts at the Vefrings. Heiler's gardener and a couple more men are in full swing. They are not digging up the weeds but the flowering bushes and trees. Mrs Olavsen watches them from the veranda, believing she must be having nightmares.

She is not dreaming. Happy as a lark, Mrs Vefring informs

her from the balcony that the vegetable beds and the currant bushes are to go. Limited cultivation of that kind is simply bad economy and in any case ought to be left to people of a simpler type, that's what they're suited to. A few of the trees are going here, others there. Will they survive? They must, or die. The old must always give way to the new, sentimentality gets you nowhere. Mrs Vefring, for her part, finds herself able to stand whole-heartedly on Torbjørn's side, now that he is finally getting the chance to exert his talents as a member of the new board of directors. As Marie knows, the struggle with this old-fashioned apartment and with the garden has always been a drawback for Mrs Vefring. A misuse of woman power. The idyllic period, with all its slovenliness and slipshod ways, is past; the time has come for realistic tasks.

'No, you weren't able to achieve the idyllic state. The garden wasn't a success, nor was Torbjørn's law practice. But I didn't know until now that failures could be dangerous to people other than themselves.'

Mrs Olavsen looks down in fury, in physical torture, at the neglected Cox's orange tree, as it is tipped over on to a cart and dragged along the ground, with bristling roots and bravely flowering branches, creaking and groaning in protest.

'You *are* overwrought, Marie, my dear. It's just as well that I'm the only person to hear you,' trills the lark from above.

The racket increases above the Olavsens' heads. One day it sounds as if a regiment of soldiers is marching incessantly up there along the bare boards. 'What on earth is it now?' says Mrs Olavsen, exhausted.

Leif looks up from his geography book. 'Erling and Odd, of course. They've each been given a pair of jackboots as a present from "Uncle Rudolf".'

Jackboots in June. A strange gift. But there is an explanation for everything. Nothing smarter, easy to put on, easy to take off, suitable for both wet and dry weather and not at all hot, as one might believe. On the contrary, light. Jackboots solve all problems to do with children's feet. Imagine, a Rudolf Heiler was necessary to find that out. Yes, that man. Notices everything, never misses the wood for the trees, incomparable. And of course it's fun to wear the same sort of thing as Father and Uncle. Marie knows what boys are like. She ought to think of getting a pair for Leif. She hopes they can't be heard too much down below?

'Not in the least,' says Marie.

A new fashion in bathing, involving large, multicoloured garden umbrellas, which kill all colours around them, yells and screams and gramophone music, evolves on the beach. The Vefrings' boys and the children from all the Heiler houses are down there, every one in jackboots, under Fritz's leadership. The rocks echo when they leap about. As if to demonstrate that jackboots will take you anywhere, they wade far out into the sea.

The Olavsens' children bathe at different times, often after sunset. But clashes cannot be avoided. Sometimes Leif comes home semi-conscious from being held under water. He forbids any intervention.

Mrs Vefring phones. 'It *can* get rather rough when so many are bathing, especially boys. But one must put oneself in the Heilers' place, no beach, cut off from the sea, and then all those growing teenagers. *Have* they a beach? Marie, Marie, an old-fashioned idyll, yes, with rushes growing far out and a muddy bottom. A bathing-house which satisfied the standards of the time, dark, sunless, with a cistern. Young people today want to bathe from an open beach, you see, they want to go from home in their bathing-suits straight into the water. One can hardly not invite the Heiler children, now that they're all such friends.'

No, of course not.

Outside, the old garden fence is creaking and groaning under the weight of Fritz Heiler, who is walking along the lowest horizontal plank. He is whistling the latest hit tune.

'I don't think you should walk on the fence, Fritz. It's not made for that, you know,' calls Augusta from above.

'Uncle Rudolf lets me, so there,' answers Fritz, tall, fifteen years old, secure, son of a rich man. 'The fence is coming down if everything goes according to plan. Had Augusta forgotten that?'

One evening Tom comes home, strangely pale, looks no one in the eyes, and is suddenly sick at the supper-table. When his mother helps him to undress, his body turns out to be blue and yellow all over.

'Tom, Tom, what have they done to you?'

Tom looks to one side and says nothing.

'Out with it, Tom.'

'I wouldn't say . . . wouldn't say that. . . .' Tom is suddenly shivering with sobs, he is only seven years old. 'They have canes, they held me. Don't ring, Mother, don't, don't, don't. . . .'

Mrs Olavsen is shaken by sobs herself, as she sits cradling the maltreated little body. Silently she points at the dark stripes when Olavsen appears in the doorway.

'I'll give those jackasses a thrashing, one after the other,' he says, white with fury.

'No!' cries Tom desperately. 'I had to promise not to tell, or they'll kill me.'

'We'll have to take it to court,' says Mrs Olavsen. 'It's the only way, legal prosecution and judgement.'

'Only at the right moment, Marie. There has to be more to it than a few youngsters fighting, and a co-tenant neglecting his garden. We need money too.'

'We should never have allowed the Vefrings to live here.'

'Augusta is part owner of the house.'

'We're like a subjugated people.'

'Yes, it's hellish, but if we admit it, then we are.'

'I can't hold out any longer.'

'Yes, Marie, we'll hold out.' Olavsen wipes his forehead.

One autumn evening he is in the part of the garden that borders on Andersson's land, busy with some new perennials he wants to try out.

'Good evening, Halvard.'

Olavsen looks up, doesn't reply. Vefring is standing there in his jackboots and an item of clothing not unlike Heiler's landed proprietor's jacket. His arms are crossed, holding the rail fence, and he has clearly been standing watching Olavsen for a while.

'Putting in new plants, I see.'

No answer.

'Have you heard that Heiler's buying to the east of Andersson, too? As far as Andersson's concerned, it's simply a question of as many as possible joining in, then he'll make up his mind. We've already been promised free right of way, as you know. The Pedersens are taking a very reasonable attitude as well. A bit of opposition from the children, but we'll soon deal with that. Now what do you say to the situation?'

'Nothing.'

'Listen, Halvard, wouldn't it be better to make peace? The times have caught up with this place. Join in and you'll profit from developments. No one ever profited from holding out alone against the current.'

'I'm not holding out alone. Nothing and nobody can alter the fact that the earth I'm standing digging in is my earth.'

'We've thought of building,' says Vefring.

'Have you, indeed?'

'We've thought of building another room on the south side.'

'It's going to hang straight out in the air then, is it?'

'No, it's going to rest on four cement pillars.'

'And they're going to stand on our steps?'

'Precisely. It's not a bad idea, I'm telling you. It'll give the house an entirely new look.'

'Yes, God knows. And you think you'll pull it off?'

'I don't know why I shouldn't.'

'But I do.'

They stand for a while, looking at each other. And Olavsen notices something that suddenly fills him with fresh courage. Vefring is tired, his face is a little puffy. He has the look of an insomniac. It even looks as if there may be something in what they say, that he's back on the bottle again. He doesn't give an impression of triumph, in spite of boots, straps and flaps.

So perhaps there's something in what they're also saying: Vefring has rowed himself out too far, has accepted more than he is capable of paying back, has given promises he cannot keep.

Well, that's his affair.

'I suppose it's too late for you to do an about turn, or I'd give you that piece of advice,' says Olavsen, continuing to dig. In a while he hears Vefring walk away.

Olavsen is still fighting for himself and his family. The story is by no means over. It is not just, but life is not just.

All the Olavsens have acquired a new expression, determined and withdrawn, something impassive that was originally foreign to them. They had open, frank faces before, happy faces, a little self-assured and gullible perhaps. They have steadied themselves with a slogan, if one can call it that, a password: if we can only hold out, they *must* give way, remember that.

And with every day that passes they love their home with a greater and more painful love.

One Day in November

It all began when I was given a rose in embarrassing circumstances. A gentleman presented me with it and said, 'Pour vous, madame.' He had searched and found one for me in a garden ravaged by autumn rain and cold weather, and it was beautiful for that time of year, a deep, velvety red, half open, and with dark, shining leaves on either side of the long stem. I shall never forget it.

The gentleman was white-haired, gallant, elegantly French. He looked at me with a humorous, kindly little smile, and I hope to this day that he did not see me very clearly, that his sight, if nothing else, was somewhat reduced. I can almost permit myself to believe it, since he did not beat a hasty retreat. He was neither tactless nor inconsiderate.

At a suitable distance behind him a servant stood waiting, with a basket in his hand, a rug over his arm, the correct and inscrutable expression and the kind of posture that only a gentleman's gentleman can possess. It was too much to hope that *he* might be suffering from poor eyesight. He was young, pitilessly young, and I caught myself thinking a shameful thought: why are you here, my friend? Why not *là-bas* – over there?

And I? At long last the sun was out again for the first time. It shone on me without mercy where I stood, as if framed behind glass in a ground-floor window, together with a red flowering geranium that I was watering. The only thing I had on was an old painting smock, so ragged that it was difficult to say which part of it was least in tatters. Round my head was a turban in the same style. And from top to toe, reaching far down my hands and high up my neck, I was coated with congealed, stinking, yellow sulphur ointment.

This was not my normal attire. But that I should have been formally presented with a rose by a strange man on that day and in that condition, is the way of the world.

It happened on a splendid, but very antiquated, very ramshackle country estate, in the middle of an overgrown garden full of venerable trees, including a cedar so huge that its horizontal branches provided a roof for a kind of open summer-house for all kinds of use: dining-room, workroom, nursery, a spacious shelter from rain as well as from sun. The walls and backcloth were tall, thick camellia bushes, which nobody pruned or clipped any more, and whose flowers were picked by no one besides ourselves, one or two swaying mimosas, and at one point a clump of bamboos, tall and delicate with their narrow leaves and thin, shining, jointed stems. For this was inland Brittany, in Île-et-Vilaine, where the winter climate resembles that of the South.

An old place, which was now rented out just as it stood, with holes in the floors, missing tiles, scurrying rats and mice. An idyll when the weather permitted, and at other times by no means a bad place of refuge for people like ourselves: my husband, our child of a few months, our maid Marie-Catherine, and myself, refugees from Paris and the innocent (as it seems now) food shortages and bombing.

It was one of those November days in France when the summer turns back and taps out of the bottom of the cornucopia flowers that have survived the autumn rain, grass that shines emerald green through the layer of yellow leaves on the ground, warmth, scents, humming insects against a sun-warmed wall; and the spare, slight shadow of the leaves at this season on gravel and lawns.

Countless times in the course of that summer I had been surprised in the window, as I sat sewing or stood painting, keeping an eye on the baby asleep outside. American soldiers, in a training-camp nearby, had appeared, two by two between the six-foot hollyhocks along the wall, had stood there with their brown boyish faces among the pink rosettes and said, 'Hullo!' And they had asked for cider and drunk it at the table under the cedar tree. If they were there for the first time they would troop up to the window again, bring out their wallets and ask, 'How much?'

But we were not running an inn and would take no payment. As time went by this resulted in friendly gifts, bars of chocolate and packets of cigarettes tossed in through the window, 'For you!'; in unexpected, cheerful shouts from behind hedges and out of ditches, when the baby and I were out walking along the road, unaware of the warlike manoeuvres going on around us, 'Hullo, baby!'; and in amused, vociferous approval the time we decided to buy the goat Cocotte. We had never owned such an animal before and had no idea how to judge it. Our American friends came along with the camp veterinary surgeon in person. He examined Cocotte and announced, 'The girl is good.'

She was too. Apart from one or two peculiarities.

At other times French soldiers would be disclosed among the hollyhocks. They came in groups of three or four and asked for Marie-Catherine, being her brothers, first and second cousins, or simply acquaintances from her village out on the Atlantic coast in Finistère. If they came from the trenches they were overgrown with beards and dirt, and brought with them masterless animals collected in abandoned towns, in no-man's-land: puppies, kittens, caged canaries. But if the soldiers came from home they were newly cut and shaved, wore clean, faded uniform jackets, and had pieces of ham, salami, round loaves of bread, everything that their families could do without, sticking out of their pockets and their *musettes* – the soldier's grey haversack. They tramped in wearing their heavy boots, sat up with us in the late evening, low-voiced, using few words, shifting their pipes from one side of their mouths to the other, and talking mostly about their people at home, their wives, small children, the animals, the tiny farm in the stony patch beside the sea, the fishing that had been in abeyance since the war began.

At night they slept on the floor with their haversacks under their heads and their greatcoats on top of them.

When they left in the morning they shook our hands with a firm grip and a last 'On les aura – we'll get them.' They said it in that slightly too high, slightly too loud voice that goes with hard times, that voice that says, I am not discouraged, never believe that. We answered in the same way, as they expected of us.

All the spring and summer I had felt more or less equal to the changing situations in the window. This time . . .

'Pour vous, madame!'

I put down the watering-can, muttered something or other, thanked him for the rose as best I could and wished the earth would swallow me up. The old gentleman was introducing himself. He was the father of our landlord, had lived here once upon a time, now seldom left his home but liked to sit once a year under the cedar tree, his favourite place since his boyhood. Illness had prevented him from coming during the summer, but today he felt well and the weather was unexpectedly clement. He came in a carriage, brought his own meals, would not on any account intrude, asked only that his servant might use the kitchen, the well, a small space at the kitchen counter, a burner on the stove; and that he might borrow one of the old garden chairs. He hoped we would be his guests at luncheon. With our permission he would unharness the horse and let it loose to graze.

'It will be a pleasure, monsieur. Thank you very much, monsieur. You are too kind.'

Seldom can anyone have been more innocent of the difficulties he was causing than that kind old gentleman who thought he had provided for everything.

I sent a bitter farewell to the hot bath that was even now being prepared for me in the kitchen and gave a last, despairing glance at the inscrutable face of the servant, rushed upstairs and put on the highest necked clothes I possessed over all the ointment. To remove it with nothing but cold water was unthinkable, and it was late morning already. I came down again with what I hoped was a natural expression suitable to a hostess and with the rose bravely pinned to my breast.

Far more important things were going to happen that day. But it all began when I, attired in sulphur ointment and rags, was given a rose.

Much is possible in wartime. It is possible to believe that you have scabies. It is no longer a thought that merits indignant rejection, nor a sign of being especially slovenly. Scabies was rife in the trenches, where the soldiers had lived for almost four years in clay and mud, among rats and lice, without a hope of keeping clean. Scabies is contagious. Anyone who housed soldiers could get it, and in such times everyone housed soldiers. The least a fairly respectable civilian could do was to give them a roof over their heads, if at all possible, while they waited for the few, irregular trains. Of course we had housed soldiers, housed them recently. The disgusting banknotes for as little as one franc, which were replacing coins to an ever-increasing extent, were also considered to be dangerous. In short. . . .

It started when Marie-Catherine came to me one day and said, 'Philomène, madame. . . .'

Philomène was the girl who looked after the farm – that is, the remains of the kitchen garden, the hens and the two pigs. It appeared that, maddened by the itch, she had leaped out of bed and rushed out of doors in the middle of the night in her shift, unheard-of behaviour in the village, had torn up nearly all the nettles behind the stables and rubbed her whole body with them like a madwoman. This had naturally not improved her condition. 'She's going out of her mind, madame,' said Marie-Catherine.

We got Philomène to go to the doctor in Redon. Since medicines were frequently not available, because they were sent to the front, she came home with old-fashioned and terrifying precautions, a drastic remedy from heaven knows what period of history. That nearly sent her out of her mind too, a state we thoroughly understood when our turn came.

Of course it did come, whether we really had caught the contagion or not. Very soon we believed it was our duty to undertake the remedy too, not least out of consideration for the child. Scabies, that cure, the delicate skin of a little child – we dared not complete the thought.

Three scalding hot baths. Between them, first soft soap, then sulphur ointment, had to be rubbed over the whole body. The soap was supposed to stay on for at least a quarter of an hour, the ointment for twenty-four hours. As far as we were concerned the quarter-hour was extended until it was possible to prepare another bath, a good while when all you have at your disposal are a well, a steaming hot cooking stove, and a tub. A good while, too, when you are dancing around naked, beside yourself with the itching. We had to produce nine adult baths after Philomène had had her three. That made twelve in all, in addition to the daily bath for the baby. We carried water, we carried wood, we got down on all fours and took turns blowing into the stove, we helped one another with soap and ointment and poured buckets of water over each other. All of it without any bashfulness on Marie-Catherine's part, which surprised us. But scabies is scabies.

Philomène walked about, cured. Fate was unkind to the rest of us; the symptoms appeared a second time. We had probably not been thorough enough; at any rate we had to pluck up courage and start again. It was a comfort that it looked as if the baby remained free of it.

This time we wore the worst rags and tatters we could lay our hands on, for the ointment ruined all our underwear. We built up the fire in the stove.

My turn came last that day. The others were ready and clothed, free to go about clean and restored. The water for my deliverance was standing over the fire, the stove was not smoking so badly as usual. I was watering the geranium . . .

'Pour vous, madame.'

As things were at that time I ought to have been able to say,

'I have scabies, unfortunately I have scabies. I have to take a bath, so your servant must stay out of the kitchen until I've finished.' But not a word did I get out, apart from a few polite phrases.

I think it was the rose that paralysed me.

The servant was already there, clattering saucepans and an old-fashioned coffee-pot, wandering across to the well and back again, to the overgrown kitchen garden, to the table under the cedar tree. He was everywhere. He limped when he walked. Perhaps he had been 'over there' and had brought back with him what many secretly hoped for, a minor disability. In that case. . . .

We could hear him chopping parsley and keeping Marie-Catherine amused.

The day began to pass. The gentlemen had been conversing for some time. Unconcerned about the tragedies of ordinary life all about them, they sat in the shade of the cedar tree, discussing the war and the likelihood of peace. Rumours which we, living so far from Paris, had few qualifications for judging, were circulating now as they had so many times before, stubborn and insistent as ever. Only a few days ago they had turned out to be false, but they persisted obstinately. What should one believe? What should one not believe?

So as not to shame my family by appearing to be an empty-headed nincompoop, I was forced to join them, moving the baby whom I did not dare pick up without gloves on, and converse as if nothing were the matter.

One of the few things that can make one absent-minded, even when the issue of war or peace is under discussion, is, I can assure you, congealed sulphur ointment. It encases the body like dead, foreign skin, and you hanker to peel it off. A snake about to slough its skin must feel the same way before it rids itself of its old, shrivelled sheath. The words I have scabies, monsieur, seemed about to fly out of my mouth every now and then like the confession of a person under torture.

I listened to the gentlemen as they moved on from the war to the weather, to this property, unfortunately gone to rack and ruin. There were no materials to be had, no workmen, everything went to the front. And they were back at the rumours again. What did they say this time? Would it really be all over before the fifth winter began?

It was being said in Paris, but what was not being said in Paris? All of us shared the countryman's scepticism towards the capital. People there were nervous, and with good reason. There they were bombed, shot at with long-distance guns, suffered food shortages. They had had the Germans at close quarters again, for the second time, as recently as the summer. Foch had driven them back again to their own frontier almost everywhere. Bulgaria had given up. Austria and Turkey. One only wished to hope, but one had hoped many times before. Yser, Champagne, Verdun, to name only the most important battles, endless sacrifice, countless human lives, an enemy front that bulged backwards and forwards, but held. . . .

The old gentleman had lost two grandchildren, his son's boys. The husband of a third grandchild was missing, nobody expected to hear any longer that he was a prisoner and alive. It was the same in nearly all families, someone gone. Clemenceau's motto had been *Jusqu'au bout*, to the end. What would the end cost? And yet – and all the same. . . .

At times I forgot my own discomfort for the ones we were talking about. At times I gave myself something to see to, Cocotte for example. She was tethered behind the house, and, tyrannical as all indispensable creatures so easily become, she would not touch a leaf or a blade of grass unless she had company. It was one of her peculiarities and sometimes resulted in a lack of milk when it was time to feed the baby. Cocotte was the cross we had to bear daily. We took it in turns to sit with her.

That day she had a horse to keep her company. She was not standing glaring in front of her as usual, but was cropping the grass peaceably, as she was supposed to do. Nevertheless I hurried to her time after time, thankful to have her to blame for it. I could at least sit there alone, while the servant came and went in the distance and delicious smells wafted over to me from the kitchen window. It was difficult to take an interest in them.

As I was sitting there the door in the garden wall opened and in came Madame Clément. She was our nearest neighbour and not our friend. We for our part found nothing to complain about, but she had the idea that she ought to have bought Cocotte and not we. This enmity was expressed in taunts hurled after us when we passed, especially the epithet 'Dirty foreigners'. Since she was carrying on feuds with others besides ourselves, and since we had public sympathy on our side, we took it calmly. This did not have the effect of mollifying Madame Clément.

Now she entered the garden, wearing her hat and shawl, with a loaded basket on her arm, muttering loudly to herself and gesticulating with her umbrella. She came, in other words, from Redon, where it was market-day, and nobody went as far as that in this area without preparing herself for all eventualities, including rain, however clear the sky.

She did not see me. She was about to hurry on when I called to her. From where I was sitting she looked more threatening than ever. I thought, whatever it is she wants, let's not have a scene under the cedar tree just now.

Then something occurred that made me tongue-tied. Madame Clément put down her basket, threw away her umbrella, approached me with open arms and embraced me. I had just managed to stammer 'I have scabies, Madame Clément, be careful!' when she embraced me again and announced, 'I don't care!' And she held me away from her at arm's length: 'I've come from Redon.'

'I can see you have, Madame Clément.'

'C'est la PAIX,' said Madame Clément. 'La PAIX!' And the tears streamed down her face. 'Peace, mon enfant, peace!'

'Is it true? Is it possible? Is it more than a rumour? Are you sure? We were fooled as recently as the day before yesterday.'

'It is true. The Germans have asked for an armistice. It has been announced from the prefecture, and the flag has been raised, and the mayor has made a speech, and everybody's beside themselves. In the church tower they're ringing the bells fit to break the ropes, they're all hanging from them, as many as can get near, one's snapped already. And the band's playing the "Marseillaise" and "Sambre-et-Meuse" and

"Madelon", and everyone's singing, and the pigs in the market-place are squealing, you never heard such a noise. Go in, and you will hear it. Imagine it happening on a market-day too, when everyone's there. I've run like a mad thing to be the first to bring the news.'

Madame Clément had run nearly four miles with her loaded basket and umbrella in order to be the first. There we stood, and dried our tears together, and if I never forget the rose, nor shall I forget that she did not go past our door that day, because joy had burnt every grudge away from her heart. Like most people she had sons at the war, but difficult as she was, easily offended and rude, it was not always remembered.

'Come and sit down, Madame Clément, have something to drink.'

'As if I've time for that! There are more of them on their way here.'

But she came with me to the cedar tree and repeated her news. The French mother announced it, and the French grandfather rose slowly to his feet, removed his hat, and at first said nothing. Then he sat down again and said, 'Thank God', while we others stood up and sat down as well.

The servant was there already with wine. Everyone drank to everyone else. We ate his lunch walking round the table, for we were all too excited to sit. We could hear Madame Clément in the distance, bringing her message farther. Her voice mingled with other voices. She herself made peace that day with large areas of the village.

Soon we were on our way to Redon, packed together in the old gentleman's carriage. That was where we were sitting when the confession suddenly flew out of me, unexpected and unmotivated, like most repressed confessions: 'I have scabies. I've caught it for the second time.' And I embarked on our tale of woe.

It made very little impression.

'Has the child had it?' asked the old gentleman finally, his thoughts quite obviously elsewhere.

'No, we've been careful.'

'Then you have not had it either. Philomène may have.'

'Why only Philomène?'

My question was drowned in the others' conversation. When I was given an answer it came unexpectedly from the servant.

'She has a young man, madame,' he said, shrugging his shoulders.

He nodded at me encouragingly, he meant well. But for someone who was sitting there stiff with congealed sulphur ointment, the thought that it might all have been imagination and entirely unnecessary was little comfort.

Peace. We thought so then.

When we were a long way off from Redon we heard a noise that we were gradually able to distinguish as horn music, singing, the squealing of pigs, ear-splitting bell-ringing and disorientated cock-crowing, for all the animals in the market-place were panic-stricken by the din. Under it all the drumbeats could be heard like pounding blood.

We had to drive a long way round to get to our destination, M. Frostin, the pharmacist. In addition to the big café in the market-place his pharmacy was the place where issues were debated. It was packed to overflowing with a motley crowd of townspeople, peasants, French soldiers on leave and Americans from the training-camp. People were coming and going, slapping each other on the back, going away to drink a glass together. In the middle of it all stood Monsieur Frostin, living up to expectations as an authority and strategist. He had taken out a large map, his finger was travelling over it, he had an answer to every question, including the most exciting, the most obvious of all: What now?

'To Berlin,' said pharmacist Frostin. 'To Berlin.'

But others were less certain, and fell quiet and thoughtful. The old gentleman said, 'We shall have those people as our neighbours in the future as well. We can't move them away from us, and we can't move away from them.' And he added something about provoking fresh dissension with one's own hands.

'Fresh dissension? That won't be our affair,' said pharmacist Frostin. 'As if we don't know them by now. Mark my words.

Those people understand only one thing – harshness.'

I myself should have liked to have gone quietly across to the public baths, in spite of past and future, now that I had come to town. But the baths were closed like everything else, except for the pharmacy and the café.

At that time I used to keep a diary about and for my little boy. When I came home I wrote: *Peace. You do not understand it and will never understand it, for war will be unthinkable when you are grown up.*

It was the 11th of November 1918.

Today the Rose

Today the rose has been kissing the orchid
  helped by the sun and the wind,
pressing its rosy lips close against
  the orchid's velvet-brown skin,
  not ceasing till after sunset.

Then the orchid quivered in its glass
  and swayed this way and that
seeking the rose which had vanished
hidden in itself and its own concerns –
  its wild, restless desire
  for new, always new orchids.

*

Such is life, sisters.
Never search for the vanished rose.
  What resembled tenderness
  may turn into hate,
and nothing is gained but loss.